"The main character in this book is a psychologist who uses past life regression to look for clues to solve a mystery in her present life. The story is set in Pittsburgh but moves to Kauai where pieces of the puzzle begin to come together. All is not as it appears on the surface and I didn't guess the ending till the final pages. This book is intriguing and hard to put down!"

Amazon review by Robin Costanzo

"The author, Cathy Corn, was adept at introducing the heroine of the story in such a human way that this reader became immediately sympathetic and interested in her life. The story moved quickly, was believable, imaginable and hard to put down...I will read more from this author and would recommend this author to other women who enjoy romantic suspense and a little Hawaiian vacation travel."

Amazon review by Kathy-Ann Becker, author of *Silencing the Women: The Witch Trials of Mary Bliss Parson*

Also by Cathy A. Corn:

BLUE MOON OVER MADAGASCAR
Lilith & the Faeries #1

SMELL THE PLUMERIAS
Lilith & the Faeries #2

FAERY: THE FINAL FRONTIER
Lilith & the Faeries #3

BEYOND THE FAERY PORTAL
Lilith & the Faeries #4

THE WITCH'S LOST LOVE

WRITE YOUR BOOK FOR A MORE AMAZING LIFE

Murder
through the
Looking-Glass

CATHY A. CORN

In memory of Walter Zalot.

And dedicated to the men and women of the contra and swing dance community of Pittsburgh. May the dance never end.

And for Princess, my first puppy. Her sweet, gentle soul inspired me and soothed away my hurts and fears.

SPICE UP your day with a FREE E-book, *Tales of the Wild & Seldom Seen*, three short stories and novel excerpt. Go to **www.CathyACorn.com** to get it (and to join my email list and learn about new releases and other free offers.)

ENJOY!

"Many people are natural clairvoyants, and after a short time of practice with a crystal ball readily see with the mind's eye impressions received in the form of a picture from within the crystal."

From *Crystal Healing, the Next Step* by Phyllis Galde

Chapter One

*L*ast night, I was jerked away from my sleep again.

I bolted upright in the blackness, eyes wide, gasping, each tortured breath bringing me back from beyond. Sweat poured off my face and torso, my heart racing. Beside my bed, the digital clock offered 4:11 to orient me to the here and now. I heard the puppy rustle and pad toward me from the end of the bed.

"Princess, come here. That was awful, the worst spell ever." My hands and body shook as well as my voice.

Ever since I moved to this house seven months ago, I've wakened at night—me, who has slept soundly all her life. Some nights I roll over and go right back to sleep. Others, I lie awake and listen to the creaks and twitches of the house and snuggle beneath the warm, safe refuge of my bedclothes.

The night terrors started several months ago, and once a week now I wake up in panic, as if my sleep took me to a faraway, haunted time. I waken feeling my life is in jeopardy, yet not remembering the dreams or even a fragment of one.

I could make out her shaggy head in the darkness as I felt her dog licks of reassurance on my hands. I petted her with long, anxious strokes until she snuggled against me, and I hugged her large, furry body to me. The terror, little by little, ebbed until I was left feeling drained.

I slept fitfully after that, my body curled around my fifty-five pound puppy, an eleven month old terrier mix. I finally rose later than usual, feeling tireder than when I'd gone to bed. My hair unkempt, my mouth a desert, I figured I must look a sight. Princess didn't seem to care, frisking beside me with a rope toy, her black shaggy coat reflecting the morning sun.

With a sigh half relief and half continuing exasperation, I turned toward the day, feeling unclean in my clammy cotton nightgown soaked through with sweat. If I weren't thirty-three years old, I'd think this was menopause.

After my shower, my mind cleared if only for briefly. Princess gazed up admiringly as I sat on the mauve bedspread of my four-poster bed and dressed. As usual, she listened attentively to my every word.

"It's fear. It's got to be that. But what am I afraid of? Not you," I said with sudden insight as I tousled her furry head. Her floppy ears perked up as I pulled on my jeans and snapped them. She knew it was her favorite time of day, and she raced downstairs.

She whacked at her blue plastic food bowl with one paw, barking loudly.

"Okay, girl. Can't say it's worth getting excited about." I poured kibble into her bowl and listened to her contented

2

crunching. I grabbed a banana, my jacket, and her leash in preparation for the morning constitutional.

"Come on, sweet puppy. A quick one in the park before I meet Sandy." I snapped on the leash while her tail flapped wildly.

I meditated on fear as I drove to my office to pick up a book I'd forgotten. Since this was my day off, I'd get to indulge in personal reading. Fortunately, the fifteen-minute drive to the office lay enroute to Shadyside, Pittsburgh, where I'd be meeting my friend Sandy for lunch and shopping.

I unlocked the glass door that read "Suzanne Westin, PhD" and stepped inside. A part of me still wondered about my waking terrors, like searching for a piece in a puzzle.

Here in this office I helped people with their problems. I've built a thriving practice as a clinical psychologist. Since I've been in practice for close to a decade, I've seen how fear can knot people up, freeze them in one small spot, and blind them to the wonders of reality.

Maybe I'd caught fear from my clients. Hadn't considered it contagious till now.

Sigmund Freud gazed somberly from a small photo on the shelving behind my desk.

"Who fixes the plumbing at the plumber's house?" I asked him, hoping he'd at least wink. Though I'd been counseled in the past, I mentally weighed the cost of some therapy for me versus my big mortgage payment. So far, the mortgage was winning.

When the phone rang, I jumped. Was Sigmund answering via my office line?

"Hello," I said, picking up against my better judgment.

"Dr. Westin, I just wanted to make sure I have the right day and time for our therapy session. This is Brad Smith." His voice, low and seductive, roused me from my thoughts. My new client this week. In spite of myself and professionalism, my heart skipped a beat.

The appointment book lay open on my desk. "It's tomorrow, Brad. 11:15. That still good?"

"That'll be great. See you then."

Something about his voice made me want to let down my long, curly brown hair, shake it out, and pull on something slinky. Clients rarely raised my pulse, even the attractive ones. I stopped in the powder room before turning out the lights.

I gazed into the mirror at brown eyes, the window to my soul, and said, "Never you mind. By tomorrow you'll be in complete control. Besides, he's probably sixty years old, overweight, picks his nose, and lives with his mother.

"I'm coming, Sandy." With a glance at the wall clock, I hastened out the door.

Sandy and I have wandered in and out of each other's lives for as long as I can remember, since grade school. We trick-or-treated together, shared about our first dates, and even kept in touch attending different colleges. We never matched externally. She stayed petite, with her fluffy, red pixie cut, and I became more willowy, with taller dark looks. But on the inside, the connection never changed. We laughed, chattered, and even howled like two small children, even though she'd transformed into a suburban mother of two, and I'd not yet married.

Sandy hailed me from a bench on the corner of Walnut Street, our meeting place. The autumn sun illuminated her red locks and stylish glasses as she sat amongst a flurry of colorful leaves at her feet. She wore jeans and a dark brown jacket that made her look like a teenager.

"Hey woman, you're looking good, there," I said.

She pointed to a wet mark on her jacket. "Peanut butter. Can't get out of the house without a battle wound."

"At least it goes with your outfit."

We embraced, and it warmed me and my semi-anxious mind. She'd always been the mother/sister of our dynamic duo, the eternal nurturer.

"Where to?" I asked. "I just want to get caught up with what's going on these days. I don't care where we shop."

"I want to get over to your new place. It sounds so perfect," she said, and pointed into an alley. "I've got to get a gift for my mother-in-law."

"Where're you taking me?" I hadn't spent much time in the alleys of Shadyside. It seemed a little...shady.

"It's a rock shop, but they have gorgeous jewelry that's reasonable. See the sign?" She pointed again, up this time, and the metal sign moved and screeched slightly with a sudden breeze that swept through the alley.

"Shadyside Gemstone Works," I read. "I'm all for jewelry. It's actually one of my addictions. Maybe I should stay out here. What's that in the window display?"

"In the back there?" Sandy's smile turned ornery, which went well with the red hair. "Isn't that what you use for your therapy sessions?"

My eyes rested softly on a colorless crystal ball about the size of a small cantaloupe amidst colorful jewelry and stones. For the past few months I'd kept running into information about crystal balls—articles, books, even a workshop that piqued my curiosity.

I couldn't resist. She'd asked for it.

"Remember how I always say you're psychic? You've done it again. Here's the manual I use for my sessions." I pulled my reading book out of my large, brown purse.

"*Crystal Ball Visions*," she read from the glossy maroon cover with its glowing crystal orb. Her eyes widened. "I was just kidding."

"So am I." I squeezed her arm. "Let's find that gift."

We walked down stairs below ground to a room like a cave holding shining treasures. The brightly lit display cases featured glittering natural stones and clusters of crystals as well as stones set as jewelry in sterling silver. Clear crystals scintillated in the light, but color predominated—deep purple amethyst, blue topaz like sunlit Caribbean waters, golden citrines like late afternoon light, deep red garnets, and much more. The words "king's treasure room" came to mind as I looked around this quiet, secluded space.

I discovered several more crystal balls, smaller and cloudier than the one in the window. Mesmerized, I stared into one that was smoky-colored.

"Could I help you?" I heard a pleasant, masculine voice from behind.

I tore myself away from the world in the ball to look at a well-groomed man with sleekly arranged salt and pepper hair, a black mustache, and a face with well-ordered features. He wore gray slacks and a black polo shirt and a diamond ring on his right pinky that flashed like some cryptic signal.

"Hello. That crystal ball in the window caught my eye. I'm afraid to ask how much it costs." I said.

"That's a natural quartz sphere that's nearly flawless. Because it's large—five and a half inches in diameter—it's seven hundred dollars."

"What about these smaller spheres?" I asked, pointing into the case at the smoky-colored one, relieved that I probably wouldn't be buying a $700 doodad that would gather dust in my house.

"The smoky quartz is $325, the clear—$350. They're three inches in diameter. Would you like to see them?"

I shook my head, but he said, "I have a few in the back that aren't as high quality. Just a minute." He disappeared with a swish behind a black curtain.

Sandra appeared from behind me and asked me to tell her fortune. I gazed at the smoky sphere and said, "A friend will fall into financial ruin after purchasing a superfluous crystal object."

"Say, Suz, what would you want a crystal ball for, anyway? I thought they were for Gypsy fortune tellers. Your book, this shop—are we having a serendipitous moment here?"

"To answer your last question first, I think so. And the ball is for scrying." Sandy looked totally mystified, so I continued. "It's an ancient practice and has been done using crystal balls, a mirror, a pool of water, and so on. When stared at under the right conditions, they can cause a flooding of images from the subconscious. You may see scenes from the past, present, or future. Scrying can be helpful in remembering past lives."

"I need help remembering my present life," she said, as our salesman emerged from behind curtain number one, sphere in hand. "Say, have you scried before?"

A trace of sadness wafted through me.

"Yes, five years ago, with a mirror. Didn't work, though. I read that you can contact those on the other side—the spirit world—by scrying," I said as he placed the three-inch clear quartz sphere in my hands.

This crystal ball suited me better than any I'd seen so far, even the one in the window. Both of my arms tingled with its energies; my hands sensed its comforting coolness. The rainbows of neon colors and formations inside attracted me magnetically. With a quick, deep breath, I experienced a moment that bordered on the mystical.

I wondered about price, suddenly in love with this crystal. "I don't understand why this one isn't high quality. It's beautiful," I said, looking at him.

He smiled as if he genuinely cared about people and not just selling rocks. "Look underneath. See that brown mark? This one is $150 because of that imperfection in the quartz and all the formations inside the stone."

My heart did a little joyous flip-flop. I examined the pea-sized, tan mark and found it barely noticeable, and I wondered at the fascinating planes within.

"Will it still work for scrying since it's not clear?" I asked.

"Some people prefer this type; others feel the clear stones are more effective. It's pretty individual and you should go by the type that appeals to you."

"I'll take it," I said, turning to Sandy. "I just saved $550, you know. Those are gorgeous."

Sandy dangled garnet earrings in the light, her mother-in-law gift.

"By the way, each one of these is crafted from a single crystal, and then worked down until it is ball-shaped." He took my Visa and transacted the sale while I tried to imagine the mammoth crystal that had given birth to the five and half inch sphere.

"I might add that the power of the crystal is magnified by this spherical shape." The rainbow tissue paper crinkled happily as he wrapped the sphere and its plastic ring stand, placed them in a turquoise bag, and handed it to me. I thanked him heartily.

With Sandy's purchase also completed, we emerged up the stairs to the radiant fall day.

Late afternoon sun gilded my wood frame house, rendering it more magical than normal. I hauled two pots of chrysanthemums to the front, admiring the purple and yellow blossoms. Standing back, I gazed upon my tan Victorian castle trimmed in rose and teal, the turret suggesting refuge for a princess. I stepped onto the generous wrap-around porch, just before the golden oak front door, and rainbow colors flashed from its beveled glass panes. I set the flowers down, pulling the bag with the crystal ball off one arm and cradled it to my chest.

A thought appeared out of the blue: *Is this house causing my sleepless nights? It all began when we moved here.*

I stepped back and shook my head. *That's a crazy thought.*

The buzzing of the ball held to my chest, my heart center, startled me. Closing my eyes, I sensed heat and vibration intensifying, spreading out to my arms and legs.

10

Maybe you're here to help me figure it out, show me the way. I shifted the stone and grabbed the bag by its handles.

We'll get started tonight.

Chapter Two

Faithful helper Princess lay sprawled on the mauve plush carpeting of our bedroom as I dusted. She breathed softly, eyes closed, feet twitching, as if she chased squirrels in her dream world.

The energies of the room were important for my success tonight. The crystal ball was resting on my oak desk, and I glanced at it as I cleaned and decluttered. I wanted my scrying efforts to work this time. A whiff of lavender incense soothed me, its smoke curling upward.

Just the dresser top and I'd be done. My collection of stones and crystals lay there, covered in dust. With pleasure, I handled each piece, some dating back to my childhood. Some unusual pieces caught my eye—a fluorite wand, a smoky quartz with orange crystals on it, a pink twinned crystal. I lingered upon a cathedral crystal, its castling motif suggesting my house in miniature.

A former boyfriend, Teddy, had accused me of being a New Age person, but I wasn't. I'd always been drawn to the treasures from the earth. As a little girl, I'd shoved stones into my pockets and dresser drawers, more content to play with them than dolls and tea sets.

After dusting Princess's baby photo, I grasped the final item—a small frame with green eyes in a happy, tan male face surrounded by a mane of curly, black hair. I wiped it off and kissed him through the glass.

"Wish you were here, Teddy. Haven't had much fun since you passed away."

The room sparkled, and Princess would be down and out for quite a while. The stage set, I glanced outside at the oak tree, its reddish rust leaves obscured by dusk.

The dark suited me best for this journey into my subconscious and going within. As the fall colors peaked, I was reminded that winter approached, another time of going within, of slowing down, meditating, and reflecting.

The incense had finished.

I settled into my comfortable office chair and lit a candle scented with rose. While the last rays of daylight illuminated the room, I slowly twirled the stone ball, identifying the formations inside: rainbows that could be an angel here, a butterfly there, another which looked like a star. The scenes fascinated me. Strong tingling extended up both arms until my jaws burned, too.

My crystal ball and I were bonding.

I spread a black silk scarf beneath its stand, as recommended by my scrying book. For once, I would do this by the book. The ball secured on the stand, I consulted the

13

paperback one last time before beginning, then turned off the lights. By now, I could barely make out the words.

A single point of light illuminated the room, the flame steady, stretching tall above the pink pillar candle on the desk before me. I touched the bottom of the sphere with my fingers, the coolness transmuting to that buzzing sensation that laid any doubts to rest. With all the electrical activity I'd experienced, I'd become a believer already.

Reason gave way to peace as I connected with the power within the natural quartz. I didn't see changes yet, but somehow tapped into the harmony of the universe. I breathed deeply and slowly to enhance my state of trance and focused my mind within the crystal ball, wiping out daily chatter and concerns. When thoughts arose, I redirected my mind to a space within the crystal.

I drifted within the heavens, floating high above everything. Carefree and detached, I experienced love, reveled in joy and peace. When the clouds rolled in, transforming the interior of the quartz, I was almost disappointed, for the serenity transcended anything in my experience, even meditation and hypnotic trance.

Then, a tiny, glowing figure appeared, growing larger until I could almost make him out. A vague feeling that I knew him grew stronger as I waited for the image to sharpen.

The flame flickered wildly now, though the air was still in the room, the windows shut against the chilly evening. Shadows danced on the walls as the motion continued, then all ceased in one final movement. The flame was blown out, its smoke noticeably acrid.

Yet a dull glowing remained in the crystal ball as the breeze caressed my shoulders, face, and neck, lingering on my lips.

"Suzanne," I heard, turning to look behind me. I could see him clearly, as if backlit, with a glow surrounding him, though the room remained dark: his black hair, green eyes, brawny chest, and bodybuilder's physique.

I felt only slight surprise, with no shock, and not a trace of doubt. This meeting seemed as natural as the day we first met six years ago.

I held out my arms. "Teddy, I've missed you so much. Come here, sweetheart."

He embraced me tightly, and with such tenderness that tears traced down my cheeks. He felt so real, so solid, just as he had in life.

He released me and I cradled his face in my hands just for a moment before kissing him gently, sensing him respond with love and fervor.

I stepped back and took a deep breath. "Ted, are you really here? Am I dreaming?"

He smiled, and I could see the love in his face. "Yes, Suzanne, I'm here, just this once. I'm allowed one visit with you. I've been trying to get in touch with you, but I couldn't get your attention until now."

"Get in touch with me?" I said.

"Your dreams, but you didn't remember anything. I tried to talk with you when you were waking up or going to sleep, but you never heard me. I even moved objects in this house, but you didn't notice. You're very involved in your work, honey," he said.

"But you're dead. How can you be here holding me and talking with me? Is everything all right?"

He took my hand and led me to the bed. We sat down together, and he put a comforting arm around my shoulders. It didn't feel like the arm of a ghost.

"Before I say anything that could upset you, let me tell you that the things in the material world that seem so bad, so awful, really aren't. Once you cross over to the spirit world you know that." He squeezed my shoulders and smiled, a familiar dimple appearing on his cheek.

"Remember how you tried to contact me after I died? You used a mirror that time, but I wasn't ready to come back yet. I had just gotten to the other side."

"Oh, I was scrying. I read about it in a book. I gazed at that mirror for hours on end, trying to reach you one last time, as the book promised. I never even thought of that when I bought the crystal ball.

"But why are you here? Are you all right?"

He smiled, and I felt so attracted to him, even though he was dead.

"I'm fine, honey. It's beautiful on the other side, more wonderful than words could ever describe. I have an exciting

16

life, full of color and light. I'm so much more alive now that I'm dead. I never feel the urge to return to this physical plane, except for now, now that I'm actually with you again.

"It was my time to go. Please understand that. I never wanted to leave you."

"It's all right. I understand." The final scene of him barely alive, on a respirator in Critical Care, flashed before my eyes. He'd been felled by a pancreatic abscess.

"Forget that, honey. I'm not here to talk about me, or even you and me. I've been trying to warn you," he said, his voice and face betraying his concern. "Your life is in great jeopardy, and this really isn't your time to die. But it could happen, anyway."

"What do you mean? I've always felt safe, and still feel that way. Who would want to hurt me?"

"You believe in past lives and reincarnation, don't you?"

I nodded.

"You have a pattern in your past connected with murders. Sometimes you were the victim, sometimes you were the murderer. This is your big opportunity to break out of that. If you don't figure out the past, you may very well be killed again."

"Who will try to kill me?"

"You have to figure it out yourself. I'm sorry, baby."

"But how? Where would I even start looking?"

He brushed a few hairs back from my face, stirring up old feelings I'd thought completely gone. "Use your crystal ball. Go

17

gazing as often as you can. It will all be revealed to you. At least you followed my suggestion to buy it."

"Your suggestion? This is the first you've contacted me."

"No, you thought it was the wind whispering in your ear, but it was me. I came to you in your dreams and even told you where to go to find a sphere, but your conscious mind has denied my visits. I've been watching over you, dear."

He seemed to fade before my eyes, then he was visible again, and he gave one last warning. "This is important. Look within yourself to break the pattern. Your life is in grave danger unless you look for answers." His solemn expression changed to mirth, and his eyes glittered with fun.

"What is it?" I asked, still aware of his well-developed sense of humor.

"We don't have sex on the other side, but we do have this other thing that's even better."

"Come on," I said. "What could that be?" We were standing by the bed and he was beginning to fade again, and I knew our time together was drawing to a close.

"Come here," he said, enveloping me in his arms. I held him, too, so that we were intertwined. "It's an incredible thing, Suzie."

A huge beam of white light surrounded us, and I experienced the peace and serenity of a sunlit summer morning. I closed my eyes and traveled in a tunnel of lights flashing brilliant rainbow colors. Haunting melodies filled my ears, and delicious aromas floated around me. The experience could have lasted hours or seconds, but the light faded, and I came back to the room. Teddy was holding me more tightly than ever, for my knees shook and my head spun.

I spoke to him fondly. "Some things never change. You're still the best, dear." He kissed my forehead, and when I opened my eyes, he'd gone.

That night, for the first time in seven months, I slept without waking.

I awoke feeling rejuvenated and more rested than I could ever remember. I kept thinking about my time with Teddy, and my morning had a peaceful, dreamlike quality to it. A nagging voice of doubt tried to intrude on this feeling of bliss, but I wouldn't listen, at least not this morning.

Though I'd gotten up early, full of energy, my attention had been on my crystal ball adventure and not on the physical world and such mundane matters as time. I returned from walking Princess and glanced at the kitchen clock: 10:45 a.m. I had a half hour to get ready and drive to work for my first appointment of the day.

With only moderate panic, I raced Princess up the stairs to the bedroom, pulling off my sweats. I threw on dark plaid dress slacks with a frilly, melon-colored blouse in an attempt to look professional. Long ago I'd given up on looking learned and wise, and instead strove to appear caring and sympathetic.

I quickly applied makeup and ran a brush through my long hair. Ready to charge off, I faced a forlorn Princess flopped on the bedroom rug, her head low between her front paws.

"Listen, young lady, I won't be gone long. Honest. We'll go for another walk tonight. Maybe James will go with us." Princess didn't look too excited, though her tail thumped ever so slightly.

Fortunately for Princess and me, the short drive to the office enabled me to come home between appointments to play with her sometimes. It rejuvenated me, and I could actually focus better on the sessions with my clients.

As I started the car, I switched into psychologist mode. I like to keep my home and work worlds separate, and now I focused on the day ahead.

I hoped my new client, Brad Smith, would wait if I was late. I prided myself on being early for sessions, especially for new clients, to make a good first impression. Trust improved the therapeutic relationship.

I navigated the two-lane roads with practiced motions, weaving through residential neighborhoods to a small business strip in Greentree. My building was located on the main drag of Greentree Road, easy to find, and a central location for most parts of the city. The parking was free, and my practice was growing steadily, as if Greentree was a sort of greenhouse for psychological counseling.

I pulled into my parking spot near the rear of the small brick house that had been converted into offices. I shared the building with a hair stylist, an insurance agent, and a dentist. The mix of service providers had encouraged me in the beginning, and even now I was glad I wasn't strictly in a medical building. It just seemed more balanced this way.

I unlocked the outer glass door and glanced at my watch: 11:11 a.m. I breathed a sigh, knowing I'd barely made it.

I felt the tiny flutters of anticipation I often experienced when waiting for a new client. It was exciting in a way, for I'd be entering a new world—the world of a unique individual— and seeing everything through his or her eyes.

I'd helped many people over the years, those with weight problems, others trying to quit smoking, people suffering depression and anxiety, among others. I'd even had good success treating men and women with relationship problems, which baffled me, since I had such a low success rate with myself. The example I set for my clients was pathetic, but fortunately, they didn't know.

I flicked on the lights in both rooms, the waiting room and my inner office, and straightened the papers on my walnut desk. I rearranged the chunk of dark purple amethyst, placing it nearer to my chair. I heard the bells jingle on the outside door, signaling the arrival of my client. I straightened my blouse and stepped out to greet him.

My eyes widened and I was temporarily at a loss for words—me, the big therapist.

21

He was absolutely gorgeous.

"Dr. Westin," he said, rising from the chair. "I'm Brad Smith, your 11:15 appointment."

I smiled weakly, surveying the even facial features, the broad smile with its boyish charm, and the penetrating blue eyes beneath a casual arrangement of brown hair.

He moved with great energy, and I noticed the ripple of his biceps and triceps as he took off his light jacket and sat down in the comfortable armchair across from me.

"You do bodybuilding?" I asked.

"Yes." Again, that smile that could drive a woman wild. I wasn't certain I was a good choice to provide therapy for him. Funny, looks didn't usually excite me, not even a handsome build or winning smile. What was inside the package attracted me more. For some odd reason, this man tugged at my heartstrings. Of course, Teddy was a bodybuilder, too, but that coincidence still didn't explain it.

After he filled out the necessary insurance forms, we talked easily together. He reiterated the problem he'd described when he had made the appointment: "I have terrible problems with my relationships with women. I can't seem to find anyone I'm compatible with. I'm coming to you now because I just lost a wonderful woman who was sweet and loving, and who told me I needed a shrink."

He looked dejected, and the fire had gone out of his charismatic face.

We talked, and the hour flew.

Throughout our session, I got the impression his answers were guarded, a veneer hiding the truth. He wasn't opening up, revealing the information I needed. Or that he needed in order to get to his problems. First session, what did I expect?

"So how many sessions do you think I'll need?" he asked as he rose and stretched.

"I can't really say at this point, but with a long-standing situation such as yours, it may take many months before you get satisfactory results. And of course, the more honest you are with yourself and me, the faster we can make progress."

"I really want help, Dr. Westin. I really want to change myself this time. I'd like to be able to hang on to a girlfriend."

"I'll be glad to delve into that again on the same day and time next week, if that's all right with you, Brad."

"Put me down, Doc," he said with that heart-stopping smile, and then he grabbed his jacket and disappeared through the doorway.

I sat at my desk, wondering what next week would bring. Here was the exception to the rule: a client who appealed to my feelings as a woman. Should I continue or send him away now? Would I be able to help him, yet maintain professional distance?

I rose and stretched, whispering "help" into the air. My date with Ted seemed years ago, and I'd returned with a thud to the real world. Bliss was history.

I ran cold water in my bathroom sink, splashing it on my reddened cheeks, careless of the makeup. Then I patted my

23

face dry, turning my thoughts to my next client, Mrs. Levine, who would be sitting in the waiting room.

Focus, dear. I tucked my shirt in and straightened my pants. *Focus.*

Chapter Three

*T*hat evening, I drove home nearly oblivious to nature's majestic display of sky a penetrating blue and sunlit trees turning jewel tones. Yes, I was going within, but almost against my will. My feeling level of the morning had burned away like the fog and dew of the meadows. Now, reality was setting in, the darker side of Ted's visit, his strong warning to me of impending doom and gloom.

I wondered if I should find someone to take Princess after I was gone.

Gone had a mighty final ring to it.

Princess greeted me at the back door, and I quickly changed into black sweats. We rushed over to Crafton Park, just a few blocks from our house, and ran wild in all directions. I sweated on our way home, despite the cool air and the filtering away of sun as evening advanced. Not only was I energized because of my possible premature death, but because of Brad's advent into my professional life.

I snacked lightly, choosing to eat later after my scrying attempt. Scrying was my top priority now after work; the faster I revealed information about these past life murders, the sooner my activities could return to normal.

The urgency gnawing at me completely opposed the scrying process itself. The more anxious I felt, the more driven my purpose, the less apt I was to ever break through to any visions. Successful scrying requires a trancelike, peaceful state.

In some ways, I wished Ted had never warned me, but I knew in my heart that it had been necessary. Ted had always had my best interests in mind. Besides, I cherished our final visit together, though I sometimes questioned whether it had happened or I'd dreamed it.

As I finished my fruit and cottage cheese at the oak dining room table, Princess turned in circles, and then settled into her fleece-lined dog bed in the living room. In minutes, gentle snoring filled the room like background music. Her antics relaxed me as I quietly treaded up the stairway, intent on my mission. I wondered if cottage cheese was a good scrying food.

I felt magnetically drawn to the object shrouded in a black silk scarf on the white wicker bedside stand. I took several slow, deep breaths before unveiling it.

Immediately, it impacted on me, as if we'd just met for the first time: a glint of light, attracting me and soothing my jangled nerves, a flash of rainbow in iridescent colors, like the promise of a beautiful beginning.

I gathered the crystal ball into my hands and held it before my chest, savoring the fine buzzing sensations. In just seconds, hope permeated my being. I knew I could overcome

26

the mountain of problems that had just materialized in my life. Without a doubt, Princess and I would have many happy years together.

These epiphanies wilted considerably after I'd gazed for what seemed like two years with no result (twenty minutes by the clock). I'd settled at my desk, used the black silk as background, lit a candle, and had used deep breathing and other relaxation techniques. I'd cleared my mind and gazed softly into the crystal ball, everything done by the book—my scrying text.

Something nudged at my leg, and I glanced down to see Mr. Baseball Bat's smiling face. Princess held the green plastic toy in her mouth and shoved him gently, her tail wagging madly, and I was grateful for the diversion. I stood up and tossed the toy with the obnoxious grin down the hall and looked around the bedroom to clear my head. With the walls darkened, I could make out the flowers on the wallpaper, but not the colors, the cream background with pink and mauve roses. The mauve hangings and spread of my four-poster bed looked dark and lifeless. The treasures on my old tall chest lay muted by the absence of light.

I continued to throw Mr. Bat until Princess tired of the game and disappeared down the stairs.

When I turned back to the desk to put away the sphere, I caught a glow from the corner of my eye. Looking straight at it now, the light had gone.

So you're teasing me now.

27

I sat once again, but hummed a song under my breath. I projected happy scenes of Princess and me into the orb. This wasn't by the book, but my maverick spirit took control. Soon I felt pulsing, and clouds rolled into view, and I switched my focus to inside the crystal ball.

A figure appeared within the sphere, glowing white. Was Ted returning? Then my awareness of the crystal ball faded as a hawk filled my senses. Wings outstretched, it circled majestically, radiating its strength and vitality. A faint cry, that reedy "kree kree" that never failed to thrill me, came through. My special bond with these winged messengers commanded my complete attention to the scene.

The hawk soared above a field that bordered a wooded area. Peace filled me, as if I'd descended into a hypnotic trance.

The clouds rolled in again to my disappointment, for I needed the vision to continue, but then another scene appeared. A Victorian house came into focus, light gray with dark blue trim. Other than the color, it looked exactly like my house. As though I had become the hawk, my view switched to overhead, showing cars on the street and what looked like a navy Desoto behind the house, like one I'd seen at an antique car show.

Every single car was old, nothing more recent than the early 1940's. I'd entered another frame of time, and the era fascinated me. When my focus returned to the house, fairly certain by now that it was my house, I experienced something new and alarming. I'd begun to sweat—beads of it formed on my forehead—and my hands were shaking, my mouth was dry. When the palpitations began, I wasn't surprised, for the fear had returned.

I held on a few minutes more, wanting to continue the scrying session. When the clouds rolled in and the sphere went blank, I released my sweaty palms from the ball, exhausted.

The hawk, the messenger, could be nothing but a good omen, as I contacted the creative energies of the crystal ball. The rest of the message pointed in a darker direction.

The danger was here, in this very house I so loved and cherished. Danger had struck me here once before and might very well strike here again. Something very bad happened here, something terrible.

I returned the crystal ball to its spot on the bedside stand, hands shaking, covering it with the black silk scarf.

Princess and I frolicked in the park the next morning, practicing her training commands, running fast and free. I couldn't run away from the danger in my life, but exercise did take the edge off the tension.

Out of breath, I stopped and drank in the surrounding beauty. The stately maples and oaks always called out to my heart, but now this sanctuary had become a cathedral. A stained glass motif vibrated in the brilliant reds, oranges, and yellows that whispered to the green carpet below. If I could just stay here in this place that felt sacred and safe, I'd be all right.

The silence was rifted by Princess, barking and yanking at the leash. A fat squirrel on an upper branch had attracted her attention. The squirrel stood its ground, scolding with loud "chit" sounds, and Princess could bark forever, so I reined her in and steered toward home. I needed to plant the mums before work, anyway.

Goodbye, perfect moment.

In just a few minutes, we were back at the house. When we'd reached the kitchen, the phone rang, and I unsnapped her leash and picked up. I was pleasantly surprised to hear the raspy voice of my old friend Jay Shaw.

We'd met several years ago when we'd crossed trails cross-country skiing. He was an eccentric in his late forties who loved to travel to exotic locations, but was always on a low budget since he also worked as little as possible. He'd abandoned his job in archaeology and now mostly worked as a tour guide on bus trips during the good weather. Most importantly, I genuinely enjoyed his companionship.

"Thank heavens you called, Jay. I was being held captive, forced to play mindless dog games."

He laughed, and I picture him standing tall and thin, his sun-streaked blondish hair falling in his face, nearly hiding his faraway blue eyes. "I didn't know you had a dog. In fact, I didn't know your phone number had changed, but you aren't going to get away that easily, girl. I found you."

I apologized and explained about the adoption of Princess and my move to the Victorian house. "I really wasn't trying to ditch you. This place has absorbed my time and energy. You know, when I first walked into this house, I felt like I'd been here before. I got a little chill." Another chill rippled through me as I realized the irony of my statement. I'd ignored the initial warning. Why hadn't I listened?

"Is that so? You know what I always say about you psychological people."

"I know, I know. We're all a little wacky. I guess I'd have to agree with that."

"But before I forget my mission, I want to invite you to the social event of the season. I'm only taking positive responses."

Any activity that could take my mind, what was left of it, off my worries sounded great. "Yes, I'll come," I said eagerly.

"What about my speech, the one I've worked up to persuade you to join me? I'm crushed. It was very eloquent."

I sank onto a kitchen chair, the smile relaxing my face. I certainly needed some comic relief, and Jay Shaw was an expert in that department. "All right. Sell me."

He explained about the swing dance on the coming weekend at Heaven, a club in downtown Pittsburgh. He offered his services as my personal escort and didn't seem at all concerned that I didn't know how to swing dance.

"Not one step," I said with great remorse.

"If you have a dress with a full, twirly skirt, then you can dance. It's all in the attire."

"Yes, I have several." Maybe there was hope for me.

"Actually, it's all in the lead. Have you ever taken ballroom dancing?"

"I took a class once with a friend. He was lost, though. I did most of the leading."

"This weekend you will float around that dance floor like a pro with my expert leading," he said. I detected a little bit of bull in his presentation, but that was Jay.

We made arrangements to meet at 9 p.m. on Saturday at Heaven. This made me wonder if I'd soon be visiting the authentic heaven, if I didn't stick to my scrying sessions and unravel the clues.

I hummed to myself, happy about this diversion. I'd go and dance away my cares, forget about the problems, and get lost in the music—sweet release.

Chapter Four

 $\mathcal{T}$ he image of the gray house with dark blue trim from my crystal vision haunted me at work, though I still listened carefully to my clients. The answer came to me as sudden inspiration during a break. If this was true, that back in time the house was gray, it should still be under there. I would look for the gray paint.

I see denial frequently in my clients, and part of me wanted to deny all this. To believe blindly without solid material evidence went against my nature. I held onto my doubt like a sacred talisman, for perhaps it could rescue me from this dilemma.

Later, out back by the detached garage, I tried to recall if this building had existed in my scrying scene. The scene unfolded in my head, including garage, and I was grateful I wouldn't need to scrape away at the house.

I found some loose curls of paint behind a bush and scraped a small area near the bottom. A can of beige paint was stored in my basement for touch up, so my act of destruction would be only temporary. I banged at the spot with the scraper, impatient to peel off seventy years of paint, and to my surprise, a chunk fell away.

As if I'd traveled back in a little paint time machine, I leaned forward and peered at an irregular opening about the size of a dime. Around it were chipped layers of various colors.

The little opening was gray.

Tingles shot throughout my body, and a kick in the solar plexus further alerted me. I straightened, and my cool, rational mind took control.

This proved the house had been gray back in time, but it didn't prove about the danger to me. And there was no evidence that the gray dated back to the 1940's. It wasn't like counting the rings on a tree stump. So much for my proof.

I extricated myself from behind the bush, standing tall and stretching toward the sunny sky laced with white, puffy clouds. I stashed the scraper in my pocket and started toward the house, when I heard the engine next door, the scrunch of tires on gravel. I turned back to see the old red Bronco pull in behind the neighboring Victorian house.

We were twin Victorians on this hill amongst our neighboring houses of other periods and styles. We weren't identical twins, for Jim's was bigger and shaped differently and painted two shades of blue. He lived alone in his huge house, too, for his father had recently died and his brother had moved away.

As James Rummel waved and came over, I admired his tall, lean frame and dark-haired good looks. I had always found him handsome, except when he told funny stories and contorted his face into strange expressions. Even then, I appreciated his wit, and he'd become my dear friend and dog walking companion in the months since I'd moved here. Granted, he did show more interest in Princess than he did in me.

"Hi, Suzanne. If we hurry, we could run over to Settler's Cabin Park before it gets dark, show Princess the great outdoors—some trees and maybe a rabbit. I can drive the Bronco."

Close up, he looked even better. I tried to restrain my smile since I didn't want to get caught lusting for my neighbor. "Great idea, buddy. I need some forest energy. Let me run in and get the furry one."

Princess was plastered against the back door, eager to escape. I tossed the paint scraper, grabbed her leash, and trailed behind as she flew out to James. He opened the passenger door, Princess leaped into the back seat, and I settled in front beside him. Before he started the engine, he flashed me his world-famous smile, the one that rendered him totally irresistible.

What was it with me and handsome men lately? James was giving my pulse a good workout, and my cheeks felt hot and telltale.

"You know, as I've already said, if you're ever busy and can't walk the pooch, I'll be glad to take over. The offer always stands." He was staring at the road, oblivious to my flustered state.

"One of these days, friend, but I owe you too much already. Princess would be excited to have a date with you, though."

James was not only handsome, but of the helpful variety of male. He was never too busy to look at a problem, fix it himself, or offer advice. He thrived on serving others. After I'd moved in next door, he'd brought me two quart jars of his homemade vegetable soup, delicately seasoned with herbs, aromatic and delicious when heated.

"So how was the brain analyzing today? Did you make any exciting breakthroughs?" He was tooling along Steubenville Pike, a short drive to the park, a silly smirk on his face.

"I thought one of my clients, an older lady, had multiple personalities, but in the middle of the session I suddenly realized it was me, instead. So at the end of the session I required the woman to pay me and my other two personalities full fee each."

"If therapy's completed three times as fast, that would be worth it. Now, come on, Suzanne, tell me something nice and juicy and real."

"Well, maybe if I change the names and circumstances to protect their identity. Let me see, I did interview a new client recently. He could be considered very physically attractive, in his mid-thirties, and he came to me because he couldn't keep a girlfriend."

"Lucky guy. If he's that charismatic, he can just romance one right after the other. What a life!" James's expression relaxed till he looked wistful.

"What about you? You've never mentioned anything about girlfriends. Do you romance one right after the other?" I'd wanted to ask him this for months, yet always hesitated. Was this the new me?

James laughed without much mirth as we pulled into the park entrance. He turned at the first picnic area, parked neatly, threw open the door, and guided Princess from the back seat by her leash.

"All locked up?" he asked before we headed across the grassy mowed hillsides. I loved the sense of space here in the park, the ancient trees with their gnarled limbs; the leaves were brightly colored here, too. The chilly air was refreshing after the heat of summer.

"If you don't want to answer my question, that's all right. That's personal territory and I don't want to trespass," I said softly.

"You know me—I hate to get serious about anything, but this relationship business has been perplexing. I've had a few girlfriends over my thirty-five years, I even lived with a woman for three years, but that was a while back.

"You women are hard to figure out."

We both turned and stared meditatively at a female of another species. A healthy-looking doe stood at the edge of the trees, the last evening beams of light illuminating her sensitive face and brown coat. We stood in silence, since Princess wrestled with a stick on James's other side and hadn't spied her yet.

I blinked and saw the deer's white tail waving at us as she leaped back to her forest haunts. Princess frantically twisted her head from side to side, but saw nothing as the doe crashed through the underbrush. I might have missed the entire scene if I'd blinked twice.

"She's beautiful," said James, stroking Princess's shaggy head, yet staring at the woods where the doe exited.

"I think it's a good omen to see a deer. I think it means good fortune."

"But not if the deer is in front of your car and you're driving," he said, his face twitching.

"Yes, that's a bad omen, a very bad omen."

We hiked about the park at a brisk pace, soaking up the woods vibes, chattering about nothing in particular. We'd nearly returned to the parking lot when James cleared his throat and smiled.

"Back to relationships, my friend. I'm curious about your history, too. With your petite figure, that dark hair that blows about your face with those doe-like brown eyes, you could take your pick, have 'em standing in line. And yet, I haven't seen any men lounging on your porch. What gives?"

I could see he'd relaxed since the spotlight was focused on me, now. I was surprised we'd gotten so personal, for we usually were silly and detached, and we had never asked these soul-baring questions. Guess I'd started it.

"In my thirty-three years, James, my love life has been one disaster merging into the next. I'm also a big fake. Here I am helping this guy with his relationships with women, and I haven't a clue myself.

"In short, I'm not very good at relationships."

"I see, and how long have you been experiencing this problem?" James bent over an imaginary notebook in his hand and scribbled in the air.

"I hope you take Blue Cross. Let's see, I lived with John, my college sweetheart, a few years. I've dated other men, but usually not longer than a year. Lately, I've been busy with my work and the house." Therapy in the great outdoors felt liberating, if only I could control my dog, who was pulling me toward the trees.

"But back to my new client, the one you think is lucky because he can have all the babes. He came asking for help, but I got the distinct impression he was withholding information. His answers were too polite and distant."

"That makes perfect sense to me. He has problems getting close to women and who does he choose but a female counselor? A very lovely one at that." James put both hands on my shoulders, wiggling his eyebrows. "Did you think he would just open up to you?"

I sighed. "Why did I need Dr. Rummel to instruct me in this matter? That makes perfect sense. I guess part of me knew that but was rejecting the idea. Anyway, most people don't open up right away. Do you think I should refer him to a male psychologist?"

James contorted his facial features, and I snorted. "What, and deny him the pleasure of allowing him to fail his therapy? Or even romancing the therapist? Sounds very intriguing and delightful. What do you think?"

"I generally get a gut feeling in the beginning about whether I can help a person or not. I'm not too far off, as a rule. And I definitely think I can help this man."

"There's your answer. Maybe ultimately you can unlock the secrets of his soul more skillfully than a male therapist who wouldn't have great legs like you.

"So do you think you can help me with my problem with women?" We had crested a grassy knoll and the brilliant red rays of sunset greeted us above the distant tree tops. James was grinning as Princess spied a rabbit, barked, and strained at her leash.

I stared at the sunset meditatively, wondering exactly what he meant by that. My cheeks felt flushed again in the cool evening air.

"I'll help you with your dilemma if you help me with mine, Dr. Rummel. Spectacular sunset."

"It's a deal, Dr. Westin." We shook hands solemnly, then burst into laughter.

"It's comforting to have a romance counselor at last," he said, and we steered Princess back toward the Bronco.

* * *

I put off scrying that evening as long as possible. When I'd bought the sphere, I'd had fantasies of Disney productions floating into consciousness, cute little bunnies and fawns traipsing through flowers. During my last session, I'd felt extreme anxiety, and fear ripped through me like a destructive storm.

I just wasn't having fun.

Yet, I had to admit, my curiosity raged. Who was I back in time? What terrible things happened to me? Like a best-selling thriller, the plot of my past life drew me on, kept me wanting to turn the next page.

Regardless of mixed feelings, the job had to be done. I lit the rose pillar candle, turned off the overhead light, fondly cradled my crystal ball, connecting with its energies immediately, and placed it atop the black silk scarf on my desk.

Princess lay flopped beside my bed, eyes closed, breathing softly, with an occasional "yip" escaping her dog lips. Could she be hunting in her dreams again? I sat composed, relaxing, meditating, and maintaining digital contact with the crystal. I was prepared to wait it out, no matter how long, as I gazed softly into the stone's depths.

Almost immediately, golden clouds rolled in, or so it seemed, and a scene unveiled itself as if I'd entered the crystal ball or perhaps the scene had jumped out to join me. I had no idea of the mechanics of my visions.

I stood in a large, darkened room, a plain rectangular space with chairs set up around its edges. Someone laughed near me and music blasted from the front of the room. Then I became aware of all the people—men and women paired off, dancing.

The clothing and hair styles struck me first, as the band charmed my ears. I had stepped back in time, judging by the styles. At the front of the room, on the stage, the band played that well-known tune, "In the Mood." Seven men wore white shirts and black slacks, playing various instruments, including two on saxophones wailing loudly. The band played with great energy, leaning into the music, and the dancers' faces were animated.

The dancing excited and appealed to me. I witnessed happy faces, turning bodies, arms pulling women in and twisting them around. The couples were heavily engaged in activity, feet and arms flying, the room filled with these couples. And all in time to the music.

I watched with a growing sense of belonging to this movement, this passionate display. Somehow, an unexpected familiarity crept into me, as if this dance were a beloved, heady perfume I inhaled.

This place, these people, this music—I tapped my feet, suddenly at home here, and yearned to grab the hand of one of these men and go for a spin (or two or three).

Chills raced up and down my spine as mists invaded the room. White clouds started to obscure this happy, energetic

42

scene. But before it all disappeared—and I wanted to stay in this place—a man approached from the midst of the crowd.

That sense of déjà vu deepened as I observed this man in his forties with a slender, sturdy build. He was balding with his remaining gray-brown hair clipped short, wore tan pants and bright red shirt opened several buttons down, and glasses. I would normally say he looked ordinary, yet I found him appealing, even highly attractive. My heart thumped as he walked straight to me and extended a hand, his smile beckoning.

"Hey, doll, want to dance?"

My excitement heightened and I smiled in return. Quickly, I reached out to him.

The mists closed in, and the scene was completely obliterated. Whoever the man was, he was gone, gone back to another place and time.

I was sitting in my office chair at my desk, my fingers still contacting the crystal ball, and my hands trembled. I became aware of Princess on the floor beside me, poking Mr. Baseball Bat into my leg.

"No, Princess," I said and stood up and stretched cramped muscles. Princess jumped up and grabbed a stuffed raccoon, running in a circle to entice me into her dog game.

I stooped down to her and petted her furry head. "I've been gone, girl. Far, far away. Even though I seemed to fit in there, I'm glad to be back. Wherever that place was, I've been

43

there before, maybe in another lifetime. I don't quite get the things I'm seeing and experiencing."

She must have understood me, for she dropped her dog toy and stared at me soulfully.

The crystal ball looked dull and lifeless now. I lifted if off my desk, the black silk swishing gently as I gathered it up, too. I returned it to its stand on the bedside table and covered it.

Just think, all that excitement, probably too much, and I had never even left the comforts of home. I sighed, touching the stone one last time through the scarf. My fingers buzzed, even now, as if the sphere were recharging, preparing for our next voyage into time and space.

I knew I had no choice but to continue, no matter where the scrying took me, no matter how frightening the events.

Scry or die. I blew a kiss toward Ted's photograph.

Chapter Five

T *his will be a day of adventure.* Princess and I pranced along the deserted sidewalk, glad that traffic was light at this hour. I'd gotten up early to squeeze in a session with a new client, so I felt a little off-kilter. Regardless, the dog walk must go on. My walking partner, on the other hand, showed no signs of stress, full of zest for her morning outing, clipping along with head held proudly erect.

Though scrying visions and fears had dominated my consciousness lately, I was growing excited about Jay's swing dance. Tonight was the night, and I'd wasted precious time this morning fiddling with my dresses, trying to nail down a final wardrobe choice.

I was humming "Chattanooga Choo Choo" when we arrived at the park. Even in the early morning light, the change was obvious. Yellows and reds illuminated the leaves of more of the trees. Leaves floated down with each capricious gust of wind, and though the fall colors charmed me, I acknowledged that tug that leaving summer behind always gave me.

No, summer, don't go. I didn't really think my wishes could influence the change of seasons, but a little moaning seemed appropriate.

Princess stood alert by my side and I knew she was ready. Whenever the park was deserted or we came early, we worked on our project. It was a source of pride and wonderment to me.

I bent down and unsnapped her leash. I closed my eyes and pictured her running across the open area toward the ball field. I opened my eyes to see her running away. I waited a minute and closed my eyes again, this time seeing her turn back and run full strength toward me.

Princess, come.

I opened my eyes just as she began barking with wild abandon. She was looking up a big oak at a well-nourished squirrel that switched its tail and made loud "chit-chit" sounds.

"It looks like you turned around and started back this way, anyway," I said, laughing. My telepathic commands could never compete with a small, juicy critter.

"I'll bet Barbara Woodhouse's dog never went for the squirrel," I told my excited pup. "I know, and I'm not Barbara Woodhouse, either."

I'd read her book about dog training and was particularly intrigued by her claim that she could control dogs by telepathic commands. I'd immediately tried it on Princess and had moderate success. My dog did seem to get the mind pictures I sent.

It was fun to experiment with it, and Princess seemed to enjoy the game, too. After the squirrel had disappeared in some hole or another, we continued our training session. Princess came to me two out of three times I called her with my mind. The last time she came to me, I nuzzled her soft head before snapping the lead back on.

"Good girl, Princess. You're a very good girl." I gave her a small dog biscuit which she chomped on with gusto. As we left the park for home, the morning fog in my head had cleared, and I felt more awake now.

"I would have missed this gorgeous morning but for you, my friend. You keep my feet firmly planted in the real world— the world of trees, earth, leaves falling, and squirrels."

She jerked her head frantically from side to side looking for the latter objects. She had a vocabulary consisting of only the truly important words.

"All gone, Princess. Time to go home, sweetie."

My mind drifted toward important matters: Which pair of shoes should I wear to the dance? Should I pull my hair back? And that all-important question many single ladies ask themselves when going somewhere new: will I meet someone? My brain predictably added the additional question: do I really want to meet someone?

"My dear, you look radiant tonight. I am made breathless by your beauty." Jay Shaw grasped my hand out in the hallway after we hung up our coats. He turned me under his arm to observe the flaring of my swishing skirt.

"Very exotic," the world traveler noted, his sandy hair in his eyes. "I may not let you dance with the other men."

I smiled. Jay was eloquent as ever and full of baloney. I caught a whiff of after shave from him—something light, not overpowering—maybe Old Spice? I eyed the Wiley Coyote T-shirt he wore loose over baggy khaki pants. We didn't look like a couple with my dressy navy print dress with full skirt. I knew this was the closest Jay got to dressing up.

"And you, my articulate friend. Your generous compliments are exceeded only by the warmth and charm of your person." I bowed low and tried to keep a straight face.

"Shall we float into the ballroom and begin our odyssey of swing fever?"

Taking his arm, we continued down the hall, coming upon the darkened room.

I drew in my breath sharply and held it.

"You all right, Suz?" Jay asked.

"I just had this weird sensation that I've been here before. Maybe I dreamed I was here last night," I said quickly, reluctant to explain my crystal visions to him.

He gave me a puzzled look as we stood till the number was finished.

The room looked nearly exactly the same as in my vision, except the clothing and hair styles were current. The dancers moved confidently, animated as before. I shook my head and experienced a tightening at my throat. How could this be?

The band wailed out the music from the front stage, with seven men in white shirts and black trousers. The saxophone player leaned back and belted out a lively tune. I listened carefully to "In the Mood" again. My throat and chest had tightened up now, and part of me wondered if I could continue the evening. Still, curiosity pestered me, and a fascination with the past interlaced with the present.

"Ready to dance this next one?" I heard Jay saying, as if from a distance. He gently took my hand.

"I guess I'm feeling a little anxious," I told him. "I'm not much of a dancer, as you know."

"Arthur Murray learned from me," said Jay, a silly little smile on his face, "so my expert lead will assuage all your fears."

"Which one led?"

"Led?"

"Yes, you or Arthur Murray?" I relaxed in the absurdity of our exchange.

"We took turns. But tonight, leave the steering to me." He whirled me onto the floor. The dance tempo had slowed down on this number.

"I don't know what to do with my feet." I felt awkward and insecure.

He showed me the basic rock step. I planted my right foot on the beat, then my left, then rocked back on my right foot, landing on my left.

"It's step, step, rock step," he said as we continued our gyrations.

Soon, I was moving together with him, my Ginger to his Fred, our movements enjoyable. In my concentration to learn the dance, I no longer dwelled on the vision. The dance filled my head, and my throat and chest opened up again.

"You must dance with some other women. Please, don't let me hold you back," I said after several dances.

"What, and let these other Neanderthal guys get their hands on you? Do you think I intend to relinquish you to some undeserving bumbler?"

"I think I'll go to the ladies' room, so please find yourself a woman who knows how to dance. I'll be right back," I said with a wave.

I automatically headed to the left front of the room, observing the dancers and their wonderful dance movements. I pushed open a door without looking up and stood transfixed.

I had navigated my way to the ladies' room without looking. How could I remember where it was when I'd never been here before?

"How did I get here?" I whispered, turning to examine the two sinks, the three stalls, and the pink décor of the room. Nothing looked familiar inside. I slumped into a chair before a long mirror, staring at myself, but not seeing me.

Shake these feelings, girl. You're here to enjoy this dance. To distract myself, I thought about Jay Shaw and our friendship of several years. He was a wonderful friend and an interesting companion. His conversations were advanced for a man; he not only talked about himself, but asked about me and my interests. He showed genuine concern and curiosity about my life. I often joked with my female friends that men could only talk about themselves, but Jay was the exception to the rule.

Despite all his positive points, Jay and I stopped this side of romance. We had never even held hands or kissed. Sometimes he gave me looks—long, lingering, smoldering gazes. Once, he'd hugged me, a hug that was earth-shattering, sexually charged, that stopped the world from turning.

After that, I avoided hugs with Jay, for though I loved him dearly and valued his company, we had progressed as far as we ever would, in my thinking. Anything more intimate felt wrong to me. Thankfully, he seemed content to accept our relationship as is.

I washed my hands at the bathroom sink, dried them, and then straightened my hair and dress. The weird feelings had subsided, and I was eager to rejoin my friend.

I merged back into the darkened room once again, aware of the excitement of the dancers. From the midst of the crowd, as if emerging from my memory, a man came.

He stared straight at me, and I saw he was balding, with glasses, and a slim build, an expectant smile on his face.

51

"Hey, doll, want to dance with me?"

The chest and throat tightness paralyzed me so that I couldn't even answer. I stood and smiled, a fixed expression on my face.

He was the man of my vision in the crystal ball the night before

Chapter Six

I gazed around the room, looking for Jay, hoping he could rescue me from this situation. Evidently, he had followed my instructions and was dancing with another woman.

I attempted a smile and said, "Do you mean me?"

He had already taken my hand and was leading me to the dance floor.

"Of course. You're a good looking dame." He smiled and looked impish.

"I don't know how to do this. This is my first dance," I blurted out as my last hope of avoiding this situation. He did look kind of cute, though.

"No problem, fair damsel. Mike is here to rescue you from your danceless distress." He deftly pushed his glasses up his nose with one finger. A large space appeared in the crowded dance floor, like a clearing in the forest.

"You know the footwork?" he asked.

"Yes. Sort of."

"Just relax and leave the rest to me."

We eased into the music, a moderate boogie-woogie number. He turned me under his arm, the navy skirt swooshing, and it felt good. He rolled me to one side, falling on one knee, his arm flung out to the far side. I held out my free arm, too, laughing. He rolled me out the other way, and we held our arms out again.

Two big hams.

Light and free, I easily followed his moves and found myself responding to this man and his expert lead. I liked him—the gentle grip he held me with—just enough pressure, but not too much. I forgot that I had seen him before—just one night before.

Dancing couldn't get much better than this.

When the music died down, he held my hand an extra minute.

"You did great, lady. You danced like a pro, but I didn't get your name."

"I'm Suzanne, Suzanne Westin. Pleased to meet you and especially dance with you. That was great. You're Mike?"

"That's the ticket. Just plain Mike." He reached into his shirt pocket, producing a white business card. "Here. I only give these out to the truly gorgeous women. My phone number. Now if you get bored or want to go for a walk or go to a movie, give me a call. I'll be glad to negotiate with you."

He winked, squeezed my hand, and disappeared into the crowd.

My heart was thumping, my emotions a strange mixture of uplifted and guarded. I slipped his business card into my pocket after glancing at it: Mike Wrobleski. So he did have a last name.

54

"What do you say? Want to do more dancing or call it a night?"

Jay appeared from behind me and grasped my hands. He brought me back to earth, grounded me from wherever I had been. I wish I knew where I had been.

Or who I had been with. Or should I say who I may have been with before?

"How about one more dance, then we'll scoot," he said, pulling me with him.

His style was entirely different from Mike's, much looser and less controlled, yet fun. I relaxed on this last number and found the dancing even more enjoyable. When the music ended, we walked off the floor until I had a sudden inspiration. I grabbed Jay's near arm and turned back to the crowded room again.

"Jay, how long has this dance been here?"

"What do you mean? Since about eight o'clock tonight, I'd say."

"I mean years. Was there dancing here during the Big Band era, when this was all first popular?"

He fingered his chin and looked thoughtful.

"I think so, Suzie. There are some photos on the walls of the old time stuff. Some of the original bands played here— Glen Miller, Tommy Dorsey. If you want to stay, we could look at the pictures when the dance is over."

"No, no need to do that. I was just curious. This entire dance and its atmosphere are like a flashback to the 1940's."

55

Tonight would be another vignette for my adventure book, yet I wondered where it was all heading. This bizarre turn of events had produced the carbon copy dance hall and the identical twin man from my vision. What could it possibly mean? My anxious, questioning mind began to feel like an old companion. Even when having fun, another part of me watched and waited for disaster to strike.

"Now, Suzie, we could go back to my house if you want, drink a little wine, have some laughs. What do you say?" Jay was asking, his demeanor charming as ever.

"I'd better get home and let the dog out. But thank you for the dance. It's been most enjoyable, as well as interesting."

He pouted, then walked me to my car.

"I guess we're doomed to being just friends forever," he said, leaning against my car.

"Anything closer wouldn't be to your advantage," I said, unlocking the door.

"How so?"

"I've heard that most of us psychologists are wacky. It might rub off on you."

"Wacky isn't so bad. You're more like zany, anyway. I'd be willing to take my chances." He held out his arms.

I slid into the car and rolled down the window.

"Good night. Add some romance, and we'd just botch up a wonderful friendship."

He was shaking his head as I drove away.

* * *

The brightly painted store front, pink and green with a mauve "Antiques" sign, had caught my eye weeks ago. It was just a half mile from my house, wedged between a ballet school and a flooring company. I hesitated, my hand on the door knob, wondering if a local store had much to offer. And I was so busy today and shouldn't be wasting time. I decided to give it a fifteen minute canvas.

The door opened easily, admitting me to a room crowded with furniture and dusty objects. I hadn't expected this attic-like effect; it had that unused room smell to it, too. My nose felt itchy and I stifled the impulse to sneeze. A few wall sconces and a floor lamp provided poor lighting. I decided one minute would be long enough to give this display of basement memorabilia.

I prepared to turn and walk back out when a screeching sound from the back regions stopped me. I hadn't seen him at his desk as he pushed back his chair and rose.

"May I help you?" he said. His face was pale with glasses; he had reddish spiked hair, an overbite, and a chubby body that reminded me of a woodchuck.

"I noticed your store and thought I'd browse." I neglected to tell him I had a large house in need of furniture. I mostly wanted to leave this crowded place.

"I'm Art Miller. Let me know if I can help you. I'll be in my office," he said. I felt relief that he wouldn't be watching me. I'd just make a quick sweep and leave.

I almost didn't see it in a dark corner flanked by wooden chairs. I tried to step back to look at it better, but stumbled against a dining room table.

What I needed most was a chest of drawers for my bedroom, and here sat the perfect answer. It looked Victorian to me, with its dark wood, oval mirror flanked by two small drawers and a marble top. Below were three large drawers just waiting to be filled with my clothes. I tried to examine it closer in the low lighting.

The chair screeched again. He must have been using a hand mirror to watch me. I had been lingering by the dresser for at least two minutes when he appeared. He explained the dresser was a local acquisition from a house sale. He acquired antique pieces from Crafton's grand old houses. When I commented that this piece was a reproduction, his face fell.

"It is, but it's very nice, and the drawers work well. It's very stylish." He knocked on the top. "This is real marble."

When I accepted his asking price of $250, his eyes widened, and he gulped noisily. I was beginning to wonder if Mr. Art Miller would ever be successful as a salesman or poker player. When he asked where I lived—the price included free delivery—the drama peaked in intensity.

"Is that the blue Victorian, then, Miss?" he asked, one eye twitching and a few beads of sweat on his brow as he wrote up a receipt for my check.

"Next door. The tan one with the teal and rose trim. Nice and close to here." I smiled and tried to understand his agitation. "I'll be home this evening, especially the early part."

He nodded and I returned home in a dreamy state, still not believing I'd found anything in that dust trap store. Princess greeted me and we played a few dog games before we raced up to the bedroom. I was pulling out sweats for the next dog walk when the back doorbell rang.

On the doorstep stood Mr. Miller, his face pale, wringing his hands. An old black van parked behind him had its side door opened, white smoke pouring from its exhaust.

"I thought I'd come while it was still light. My mother always warned us kids not to come near your place when we were growing up. I figured I'd be okay during the daylight." His eyes peered around me and up at the second story while he talked.

"But why?" I asked, pinching my hand so I wouldn't laugh.

"Ghosts," he said, looking more intense and dead serious than ever. "She just told us bad things happened here, and there were ghosts."

With remarkable speed and grace, possibly inspired by the spirits hiding in dark corners, Mr. Miller lugged the dresser upstairs to the front bedroom. I followed and asked him to move the old dresser in my bedroom to the spare bedroom. I heard a few grunts and curses before he reappeared in the living room.

He solemnly shook my hand. His grip was only slightly clammy, though he wasted no time in moving to the back door. He paused a few heartbeats to say his farewell, and then disappeared with a slam of the door. Two seconds later, he gunned the van, which screeched down the road.

I fell helpless on the rug beside Princess, laughing until I felt weak.

"I do believe our antique dealer was mighty anxious to unload that dresser. I must have paid too much." I alternately stroked Princess's silky, droopy ears and wiped my tears of laughter away.

Later, I examined the dresser more closely, noticing the dark wood was a veneer, that the bric-a-brac outlining the drawers had missing pieces, and the finish looked reddish and muddy.

But the drawers did move easily, and I loved the oval mirror and the gray and white marble top. Princess sniffed at it carefully as I went over the piece in good lighting.

I straightened, remembering Mr. Miller's anxiety, his talk of ghosts. Had he been afraid I'd return the dresser or had he really believed in evil spirits? Now that the hilarity of the situation had passed, I focused on his anxiety. Ted's warning, my scrying vision about this house, and now Mr. Art Miller's childhood memories all seemed to fit together.

Bad things happened here, he'd said.

"Have you witnessed any interesting scenes?" I asked the dresser. "Do you know any secrets?" Of course, my new but old dresser had just arrived to this Victorian manse. How could it know the house's secrets?

I opened out the small drawer on the left, then on the right, spying that small white slip of paper that could only come from a fortune cookie. I consider these fortunes to be powerful tools of divination. I turned it over and read, "All is not what it seems to be."

When Princess arrived with Mr. Baseball Bat, I felt relieved to return to mindless activity, to forget about all the complications living in this house had offered.

Chapter Seven

*T*he next week sped by with my busy work schedule, a few new clients appearing from nowhere, and my duties at home. I felt fortunate, since I loved my work and my home life and looked forward to each in their proper proportions. Since I'd bought the antique dresser and since I'd met Mike at the swing dance, though, one thing had completely changed. All my progress in scrying had come to a halt, for no matter how hard I tried or how hard I tried not to try, my crystal sphere was blank.

This distressed me despite my doubts about this danger business. My blank crystal ball convinced me more than ever that the peril was real and that time ticking away could bring my unfortunate end. I needed to find the answers as quickly as possible, though I knew more than one scrying session per day would be counterproductive.

I tried to relax; maybe I was too busy, maybe that was the problem. This morning I sat at my antique oak dining room table and sipped herbal tea. I held the warm mug in both hands, savoring the heat and the scents of mint. The tea included chamomile and other herbs to calm me, and I hoped it would calm me fast.

Despite my worries, I was aware of the tiffany-inspired lamp hanging overhead, its light shining softly down around me. Touches of color and warmth spread throughout the dining room, over the entire house, too. Contentment grew in me as I cherished this perfect moment of peace—just me and my tea.

The days were shortening, and I'd seen my first snowflake that morning in the park, yet I didn't fear the approach of winter. My life was too full and rewarding for that. This house and Princess rounded out my personal life, meager as it might seem at times. I treated Princess like my child, though some would fault me for that, but to me she felt like family.

These moments of contentment and happiness restored me as I forgot about the new fears and dangers surrounding me, coexisting with my happy, productive life.

Loud knocking at my front door intruded on my reverie. I turned and stood to see a dark shadow through the beveled glass pane of the oak front door.

I threw open the door, and he was standing there, grinning.

"It's the famous James smile," I teased and motioned for him to come in.

"Famous for what?" he asked, and came in.

"It's that scintillating, effervescent sort of smile that can launch ships or set gardens to growing." James and I often had ridiculous conversations.

"I must not have smiled on my garden, then, because all it grew was weeds—big, beautiful weeds."

"Well, then, my tall and talented friend, what brings you over to the twin Victorian?"

"Believe it or not, I wasn't doing anything special, so I wondered if you and Princess would like to..." He paused dramatically.

"Go for a walk," I guessed. Princess got up and began to wag her tail.

"How did you know?"

"Psychic. Great idea. I have about an hour before I have to get ready to go out tonight."

He raised his eyebrows, but I decided to let him wonder. I grabbed a gray fleece jacket, tossing it over my Looney Tunes T-shirt and black leggings.

"I would have worn mine if I'd known," he said, pointing to my shirt. We'd discovered we owned the same T-shirt, complete with smiling cartoon characters.

"I still think it's an odd coincidence, these matching shirts," I said, retrieving the dog's leash.

"There are no coincidences," he said in a wise tone. "And one Looney Tune deserves another."

The fresh air felt good on my face and I inhaled it and felt rejuvenated. Though the sky was overcast, the remaining splashes of bright leaf color cheered up the landscape. We quickly reached the park, and I looked up at the tall, stately trees with their graceful, beckoning limbs far above the grassy lawn. Their presence always inspired me, and I rarely failed to be aware of them, the park sentinels.

James smiled at me, then was pulled forward as Princess barked at a squirrel and jerked at the leash.

"Say, I have a great idea," I said, no longer wanting to seem mysterious, especially since he hadn't asked about my evening plans. "Why don't you come with me to the swing dance tonight?"

He was turned the other way, but I saw his body stiffen. A few seconds ticked away, and he hadn't answered.

"It's not a date or anything. We'd just be buddies," I said. Did he think I was making moves on him?

He turned around, a strange, undecipherable mixture of emotion on his face.

"It's not that, Suzanne. The last time I tried swing dancing, I made a fool out of myself. I was totally uncoordinated, and I hate to even think about it. The memories are all unpleasant."

"I'm sorry. I won't mention it again," I said. He seemed totally out of character.

"No harm done," he said, flipping into his normal, carefree mode. "So tell me, what juicy work stories do you have today?"

"Now let me see." I was having trouble focusing on clients, still shaken by his unusual reaction. "I guess it would be the bodybuilder guy who can't have relationships with women. He still isn't getting to the heart of the matter, but

65

eventually he'll work into that. He talked about working on his car today."

"Working on his car? You mean he's paying you oodles of bucks for that?"

"And I can't even advise him on car repairs. It must be the best he can do right now. At least he's talking. Sometimes there are long silences in therapy sessions. So today I learned about changing the oil in his Camaro."

"Doesn't he ever talk about what went wrong, what happened between him and the women?" His curiosity was genuine, his tone compassionate.

"He talks all around it. But something pretty radical happened between him and the last girlfriend. He just hints at it. I wish I could talk to the girlfriend. But that's not how it's done."

"I'm sure he wanted only the best for her," he said absently.

"But what about you? How's life out at the airport?"

James launched a litany of U.S. Air stories. He'd worked at the airport at his $7 per hour job for several years now. Before that, he'd worked at Beecham Laboratories in the mail room. And he could tune pianos and was trained as a massage therapist. Currently, he was trying to locate and learn to play Irish bagpipes, not to be confused with Scottish bagpipes. Like my friend Jay, his interests were unusual, and he'd not found it necessary to pursue a strictly mainstream path. Sometimes I envied their lifestyles.

As I nodded and listened to a lecture on the Irish bagpipes, we meandered back home. We'd talked for nearly an hour, rather, James had talked and I had uh-huhed at appropriate spots. I noted that therapists should find friends who liked to listen. I listened intently during counseling sessions for long hours, so occasionally it might be therapeutic for me to talk.

I thanked him for joining us as he stooped down and gave a few last loving caresses to Princess. She panted slightly and stared lovingly into his eyes.

"Have a great time at your dance. Wish I weren't such a clumsy dancer myself," he said, then strode to the twin Victorian, disappearing through the back door.

We lingered out front just a minute, and I wondered about my friend James, how wholesome he seemed, a boy scout of a guy. He'd acted oddly about the swing dancing, and for some reason, maybe intuition, I wasn't convinced by his explanation.

You're painting it all too darkly, I thought, and began to mentally run through my closet again for an outfit for the swing dance tonight.

My fairytale bedroom was lit up like a carousel, romantic music pouring out of my stereo, and I felt that excitement a new adventure invites. Technically, it wasn't my first swing dance, but it was my first solo appearance at one. I needed the diversion, and I hoped the activity would stimulate my scrying powers.

Princess lay by the bed giving me mournful looks. She'd tapped into her abilities of dog divination and realized I'd be leaving soon. The dress up clothes might have been the tip off, plus the pungent smell of ginger-lime body spray I'd spritzed with abandon.

"I'll be back soon, girl. You won't even miss me," I said, as she lifted her head, eyes bright and alert. As usual, the guilt was overwhelming, but I needed a life beyond work and these walls.

I turned to check the twirl of my short, full red skirt. It shot way out, perfect dancing attire. The men liked to get a glimpse of legs, I'd noticed in my last episode of swing dancing.

"Be a good girl," I said, kissing Princess on the top of her shaggy-haired head. I escaped quickly out back before I could absorb any more morose looks.

The dance tonight was at Wightman School in Squirrel Hill, on the other side of Pittsburgh. I'd been there once a few years ago, so I didn't think I'd get too lost. With one wrong turn and a map consultation, I found myself pulling past the school and parking a short walk up the street.

I pulled my lined black raincoat snug around me. The air was chilly, promising snow soon. While the residential neighborhood of older brick homes was cheerful, with lights warming the windows, the street was deserted and hushed.

I wondered exactly why I was here. After so many years of not caring if I met anyone, could it be that? Would I meet someone? I felt a strong attraction to this dancing and the era it represented, but what else brought me to this building? Butterflies flitted in my stomach, my childlike excitement surfacing.

I walked up the front steps of the old brick school, read the sign directing me to the third floor auditorium, swung the front door wide, and ascended many flights of stairs. I was already warmed up for dancing when I approached the door of the auditorium. I heard the music first and felt a quickening of the heart, as well as my entire energy level boost a few notches.

"Just follow their lead," I reminded myself as I slid into the darkened room. I felt confident, though I had no Jay to keep me company tonight.

As before, the space was filled with whirling bodies. The sense of motion was dizzying. I paid my six dollars at the door and walked around the perimeter of the room. The band was on stage, four older gentlemen and a younger bearded man.

I waited expectantly. In the dark, it was hard to make out the other dancers, but I didn't see anyone I knew. Actually, I hadn't expected to know anyone, but I felt reluctant to ask a total stranger to dance.

The song ended, and I tried to look available, but not desperate. A tall man about thirty-five with dark brown fluffy hair and black glasses appeared from across the room holding out a hand.

"Care to dance?" he asked, and I nodded with enthusiasm and relief, for I'd wondered if I'd sit out the entire dance.

His name was Fred, and he didn't care that I was a novice. The band geared up again, this time a fast number, and I felt my confidence shrivel. Fast songs were harder.

In a very flowing style, Fred led me into a series of twisting arm movements and turns. Concentrating on his lead, I forgot my fear. Soon I was moving in sync with him, laughing at his interesting moves. When the song ended, I felt disappointed, for I wanted more of our poetic motions; the song had flown by too quickly.

"Thank you, Fred," I said, not really wanting to relinquish him. He nodded happily, looking pleased, wiping sweat from his brow before moving away. At these dances couples danced once together, then found other partners. It seemed the unwritten rule.

Coming toward me was someone I recognized from the other dance. Walter stood tall with shoulders broad, presumably from lifting weights. In the darkness I could tell he was balding with dark hair. He extended one hand and asked, "Dance?" I gratefully accepted his offer and whirled back into the music.

Walter led me through an entirely different set of moves from Fred's. By the time the dance ended, I was feeling fluent in swing. When I thanked him, he doubled over in a courtly bow.

I felt a tap on my shoulder. I turned, then drew my breath in quickly.

"Listen, you're the best looking dame here tonight. Look at you with that short red skirt and those great legs. I hope you'll dance with me," he said ardently.

The initial shock had worn off. Here stood Mike, the Mike I had met at my first swing dance. The Mike who looked exactly like the man in my vision from the crystal ball. I felt confused when I was around him.

He wore a blue and yellow Hawaiian print cotton shirt with short sleeves. His voice sounded low and sexy, I noticed in spite of my confusion.

"I would be delighted to dance with you," I said. I could feel a smile warming the tension out of my face.

The beat was slow and sultry. He slid me before him, then behind him, his hands lingering on my arms and hands, my waist. I forgot to be awkward, awakened by his touch. I flowed with him, and we didn't laugh this time. We merely wore dreamy smiles as we danced this dance of seduction.

He held me once very close, very near, as the music beat on, and my heart beat on, and I felt his heart beating, too, through the Hawaiian shirt. I felt his stare and turned to meet it, and as our eyes melted together, my apprehension evaporated. I felt so attracted to this man, as I hadn't felt in many years.

The gaze from his brown eyes steadied me, then he turned me under one arm and the magic spell was broken. We were moving again.

The music stopped, but Mike held my hand as he wiped his brow with a handkerchief from the other hand.

"Listen, lady, I've been sitting home waiting for you to call. I had to give up my normal social activities. Now I'm sort of wasting away. How about we get a cup of coffee or something? Start small, maybe work up to something big."

Our dance together had decided the issue. I felt some kind of bond with this man, whoever he was.

"Sure, Mike," I heard myself saying, "a cup of coffee would be nice."

"Next weekend, then?"

I nodded.

He wrote my phone number of the back of his business card, stuffing it back in his shirt pocket, and the thing I had dreaded was arranged, and I wasn't sure if I felt happy or tense.

The dance moved on, and I with it, but the rest of the evening I danced in reverie, my mood altered by my intimate dance with Mike.

At home that night, I threw my red skirt and black print top on the bed. I snuggled into my long peach terrycloth bathrobe. Princess helped me change my clothes by following my every move.

"It was an interesting dance, pup." I patted her head as she gazed up at me appreciatively. "I'm dancing much better already. I'm not sure about this Mike character, but at least someone showed an interest."

I felt restless, energized by the dancing and perplexed about Mike. Did I actually have feelings for him, or was it merely the dancing? Would he provide clues to my past, or was there no connection at all?

I had to give it another try, for every day provided another opportunity for contact with my subconscious. Yes, I hadn't received any information for a week now, but I couldn't give up.

I dared not stop trying to scry. My life depended on it.

I grabbed up the sphere and its black silk covering from the bedside stand, settling on the bed for a change, the silk underneath. Here's the answer to my questions about Mike, I thought. This is where I first saw him. Please give me answers, I begged.

I felt the void of the past week and tried not to think my gazing would bring nothing. I sat in the dark, my hands almost touching the sphere, but not quite. Long, thoughtful breaths into my abdomen replaced my fear with peace, the deep peace that comes from contacting the center of one's essence. I felt a glowing of my entire being, a tingling throughout my body, and as my last fear and negative expectation dropped away, my hands heated up until they felt almost uncomfortable.

73

Then, I realized my eyes were closed; I was looking within myself and not gazing into the sphere. I dropped my chin down and gently raised my lids. My crystal ball looked fluorescent bright in the blackened room, with swirling blue mists. I caught my breath, for the quality of this session was so different from the ones before. It was more vivid, more alive, almost wild and free in character.

Beyond the blue mists, I could see a powerful healing spot, for the earth offers such magical places if we only seek them out. Suddenly, I was there, beside a waterfall, the mountain water rushing to meet a tranquil pool. The air felt cool and rejuvenating, the mists fresh and wet against my skin.

I inhaled deeply, smelling the heady scents of rose and jasmine and became aware of these flowering bushes ringing the pool: red and peach roses, and jasmine with creamy blossoms. A healing green, the pool looked bottomless, and I was reminded of my subconscious mind, the pool I hoped to tap into to find my truth.

I heard the reedy cry of a hawk. As I tilted my head back, I saw a double rainbow in the mists beside the thundering waterfall. Overhead, the red-tailed hawk circled, soaring effortlessly.

My attention switched to the powerful bird, yet when the waterfall's roar gradually faded away, I looked down again. I was seeing inside my house, yet it wasn't my house. Dark

74

patterned wallpaper decorated the living and dining room area, dark yellow with large purple flowers. I shuddered.

The furniture was all different, darker and heavier. A girl in her late twenties sat at the large dining table, writing on papers. Her long, straight blonde hair kept falling in her eyes as she concentrated on her work.

She stood up, small and lithe, her hair fanning behind her, a green and pink patterned dress moving with her. As she ascended the stairs, I suddenly realized as if she had written it on her papers:

The girl with the blonde hair was me.

I almost stopped watching, so great was the shock. This blonde woman was me in a past lifetime, I was sure of it. I followed her movements with intensity, waiting for some sign. What had I to learn from this lifetime? What was the message? And most of all, what became of this girl; what became of me?

The blonde woman went up to my bedroom, which looked different from mine in furnishings and again dark flowered wallpaper, this time gold flowers on a deep purple background. She walked over to the chest of drawers, and *it was my chest of drawers.*

It looked like the dresser I'd just bought from Mr. Miller, exact in every detail, but newer.

She brushed her hair, carefully to its ends, then peered into the mirror of the dresser, putting on makeup. She adjusted her full-skirted dress, slipped into sturdy black pumps with an ankle strap, then skipped back down the stairs.

I followed her until she was outside, out back behind the house. A car was pulling up, the navy car, looking more like a boat than a car. I saw a hand waving through the open window. I caught a glimpse of him as she rushed over, yanked open the car door, and jumped in.

It was the man who looked like Mike.

When the clouds rolled in, I felt relieved, for my session had been so intense. There was information to process—me as a blonde woman in the 40's attached to a Mike guy. Was he my boyfriend, my husband, my lover? Though there was much to absorb, I realized it wasn't enough. I needed a lot more information to learn about my murderous past.

I abandoned the crystal ball on the bedspread and joined Princess, who slept beside the bed on the floor. She awoke immediately as I gathered her in my arms, holding her for dear life. She licked my hands and face, whatever she could reach, and I felt comforted. For the moment, in this place, I was safe.

Chapter Eight

*W*inter would soon be settling into our Pennsylvania hills, and as much as I enjoyed the brilliant fall color, I dragged my feet at what came next. The Farmer's Almanac predicted a mild winter, but the wooly worms seemed extra wooly this year, and Princess had grown a thick undercoat of fur.

I sat in my Greentree office counting the goose bumps on my arms, though I kept the thermostat at a comfortable temperature for clients who sat and talked. When the temperature first dropped and the winds bit into exposed skin, I just couldn't get warm.

I leaned forward at my desk, smelling the one pink rose in a bud vase. My admirer was me—I enjoyed the energy of cut flowers and felt it benefited my clients, especially now when gardens were bare. This partially opened rose blossom had a sweet, small scent, and I inhaled deeply of it, rejuvenating myself between clients.

My office décor uplifted me, too, for I'd used good quality furniture and prints of foreign locations like Stonehenge on the cream walls. My waiting room featured walnut chairs upholstered in green velvet, and peach and forest green velvet upholstered chairs flanked my walnut desk and gray office chair with Berber carpeting throughout.

My morning had been busy, and I was thankful my schedule was full. I worked during the day and sometimes into the evenings to accommodate my clients' schedules. I hoped the winter weather wouldn't encourage cancellations due to bad roads, colds, or flu.

Being busy was especially important now, not only to pay my mortgage, but to keep my worries at bay. My office provided a cheerful atmosphere where I focused on the trials and tribulations of others, forgetting the impending doom of my own life. The rose reminded me of my last scrying session, of the rose and jasmine bushes around the pool. Rose opened the heart, and jasmine healed old heart wounds. However, I reminded myself, this healed heart wouldn't do me much good if I was deceased.

I felt a fluttering about the heart regions as I anticipated my next client, even visited my bathroom to check my makeup and give my hair a quick brush.

The outer door tinkled, and I knew he'd come. He was always five minutes early. He'd been in sessions a month now without missing a weekly visit. He'd sat by my desk looking gorgeous, his blue eyes blazing sincerity.

But he rarely touched anything of emotional content. His past and his present feelings were a mystery. I was beginning to think I couldn't help him. After all, with my history of disastrous entanglements, what did I know?

78

However, I was a trained therapist, and a dedicated one, and my own shortcomings should not prevent me from helping him. At least I could empathize with his misery.

"Come on in, Brad," I said from the doorway. He sat in a chair resplendent in jeans and jean jacket. He smiled and I recognized the familiar tug at my heart—subtle, but predictably there.

No wonder I'm attracted to him. My mind chattered as we walked into my inner office. He couldn't do relationships. I always picked guys who couldn't do relationships. This guy would be perfect.

"I'm seeing someone now. I just met her two weeks ago, and I've seen her every weekend. Her name is Janet," he offered.

"That's wonderful, Brad. I'm very happy for you. How are you feeling about all this?"

"I'm happy because she's a nice woman and I enjoy being with her. She has a great sense of humor, and I especially enjoy the physical side of the relationship."

"Anything else? Any feelings not so positive?" I held my breath and waited. This was an important moment.

"You mean like feeling scared?"

I nodded.

"Yes, I've felt scared. Here I am already falling in love with this woman I barely know, and I don't know how long it will last. According to my past record, it won't be long."

I inhaled deeply and overcame the impulse to stand up and applaud. Brad had actually spoken of his emotions.

"That's true, Brad, that your past record has been poor, but you cared enough about it to come for therapy. With the help of a therapist, you can unravel the mystery that has been your past relationships with women. We'll talk about it today and continue to do so until you are making headway or no longer desire therapy.

"I'd say your chances are better than ever to have a meaningful relationship with a woman."

Brad smiled uncertainly, interlacing his fingers and stretching.

After that, he closed back up, keeping his feelings to himself, or perhaps it was because he was so out of touch with his feelings—mysterious territory.

We talked of other matters, then, until I said, "I see our time is up. I'll look forward to our next session." I smiled confidently as he stood up and I followed him to the doorway.

"I just hope it doesn't happen again, Dr. Westin." He stared at the ground as though ashamed.

"What do you mean?"

"Nothing."

"I think this will be a good starting point for your next session," I said, really wondering what the revelation would be. I didn't know if I could wait a week to find out.

"Sure, Doc," he said, and his sheepish expression gave him away again. He was hoping I'd forget about his verbal slip, I was willing to bet.

I paced the living room, Princess following, as I waited for Mike to arrive.

"This doesn't feel like a very good idea, girl. I shouldn't have let him come here. I should have met him somewhere."

Our phone conversation a few days before had unfolded smoothly—he led and I followed. Before I knew it, I was giving directions to my house, something I never permit on the first date.

Even though I was some kind of communications expert, he had maneuvered me into this situation, and it just didn't seem comfortable. I felt slightly wooden, and the situation gave me sensations of unreality. Was I depressed about dating Mike?

We heard a vehicle pull up out back, its headlights beaming into the kitchen. Princess barked steadily until I hushed her. I grabbed my light winter coat, wrapping it around my mauve cotton sweater and jeans.

"I've got to hurry, Princess. See you later." I kissed her head.

I rushed out the back door, slamming it. Mike was halfway between his truck and the back door. Snowflakes swirled—big, fluffy ones—the motion giving it all a carnival

81

appearance. I buttoned my black coat and flashed a brave smile at him.

"We're not in any hurry, surely, Suzanne. It's just coffee and a stroll." Mike readjusted his brown cowboy hat, coordinating nicely with tan pants, a brown suede jacket, and a puzzled expression.

"I guess I'm anxious to get out of the house. Do you mind if we get going?"

"No, not at all. I just thought with the snow falling and the chill in the air you might prefer to stay here."

Now he wants to see my house—the inside, no less. Warning bells clanged in my head, but I tried not to listen.

"Let's start over, Mike." I backed up to the back porch. "Hi, Mike. It's great to see you. Where are we going?"

"All right, fair lady. We'll take off and good evening to you. What a wonderful treat to behold your countenance, not to mention other parts of your anatomy." He bowed low, and I knew I was being snowed in two ways simultaneously.

"Nice truck," I said and slid into the passenger side. "The red's brilliant. Very cheerful."

"No comments about red and Freud and sex, Ms. Psychologist. I just happen to like this color. Besides, it was marked down, too." He started up the truck and moved onto the small street behind my property.

As a reflex action, I looked up at James's house next door—looking, but not really looking. Did I see a flash of

82

movement in an upstairs window? Or was it my apprehensive self imagining it?

"I'm really going to show you coffee like you've never had coffee before," Mike said, driving through Crafton, familiar with the route.

"Where are we going?"

"You'll see. To the place where the elite go, where the coffee beans are richer, fuller, and more flavorful."

"Sounds like we're going to some South American mountain, occupied by some little dark-skinned guy and his donkey."

"Almost." Mike wheeled us onto the parkway, and I felt comfortable in his presence, though I hadn't thought so. I could almost forget I had gazed at his twin image in my crystal ball.

Almost, but not quite.

"I don't know much about you, Suzanne, except you're attractive and fun. Tell me about your work."

"I steal trucks, especially red ones."

He gave me a long, sideways stare, and I feared we'd have an accident on the parkway.

"All right, I told you I was a psychologist. I've a private practice in Greentree. I counsel people with depression, weight and smoking problems, relationship problems, whatever I can help them with. I like the work."

"So who counsels you?"

"I get together with a peer occasionally, but basically I'm uncounseled. Of course I've had some therapy in the past."

"Greentree. We're going to be passing right by there. You could show me your office."

"Could I pass on that? I get enough of seeing my office." I felt uncomfortable that he was coming too close too soon. No more invading my space tonight.

"On to the coffee, then." He smiled, but I saw a determined set to his jaw.

There was more to Mike than I'd first imagined. I liked his low, sexy voice and the tilt of his cowboy hat, and he wore his clothes well.

But chances were that he was totally unsuitable for me or anyone else if I was attracted to him. I only got involved with men who had little to offer me or disappeared quickly into the sunset.

Without me.

"We're here. It's the coffee capital of the universe. Come along," he said after parking the truck along a busy street of shops, parked vehicles, and shoppers.

"So Squirrel Hill ranks as the premier coffee drinking hole of Pittsburgh. I never knew that."

"You don't think you can get decent java where you live, do you? Once you taste this stuff, I won't have to explain any more. Shall we?" He motioned toward the sidewalk.

We exited the truck, so bright red that it represented a ruby of a truck. Just to my right the object of our odyssey lay—the Java Works, a pleasant shop painted shades of green on the outside.

I held the door for Mike as the snowflakes continued to whirl like shreds of lace, the cold teasing my face.

The coffee aroma filled me as I stepped inside, a rich, exotic blend that transported me to some mountainside. The little dark wooden tables and chairs inside sat empty except for a young woman with long, dark hair reading a book. I instantly liked the quiet atmosphere here tonight, though I wondered if Mike and I had much to converse about. A movie date was always safest for the first time out.

"What kind would you like?" He pointed to a large sign on the wall with many choices.

"Could I help you?" asked the store person, a young woman with highlighted hair pulled back and round black glasses.

Mike ordered his coffee, then turned to me. His jaw dropped an inch when I said, "I'll take hot chocolate."

"In case you're wondering, I don't drink coffee. Occasionally I have a cup of decaf, but mostly I drink herbal tea," I said.

"I can't believe I've been blithering on about coffee, and you don't even drink it. You could have told me, Suzanne." He sounded irritated.

"I like it here. I looked forward to coming. It's always fun to see new places in the city, and this is an interesting shop."

The girl brought our beverages, then we selected a table near the window. We hung our coats on the back of our chairs.

"I told you about me, so it's your turn, Mike. Tell me about your work." The hot chocolate was rich, but scalding. I blew on its surface.

"I used to work at a radio station, but the past few years I've been doing market research for some corporations."

"You mean you stand at the mall with a clipboard and ask people questions?"

"Telephone work. I spend long hours on the telephone."

"I can see some similarities in our work—you talk to people and I listen to them. The world needs its balance."

We drank from steaming mugs—the hot chocolate was not too sweet with a rich chocolate, heavenly flavor—and talked quietly. Somewhere in the midst of our conversation, I realized the woman with the book had disappeared. The shoppers passing by the window were sparse now.

"I guess we've been here a while," I said, looking around.

He eyeballed his wrist watch. "A couple of hours, I'd say. Unless you want to help sweep the floor, I guess we'd better go." He nodded toward the counter person who was diplomatically upending the chairs and setting them on the table tops.

"There's no hurry," she said. "I'll be here another half hour cleaning everything up."

"I should really go. I like your coffee shop, even if I don't drink coffee. The hot chocolate was dazzling," I said, standing and pulling on my coat. Mike had already donned the suede jacket and hat.

"I'll take you home," he said.

The drive home was quiet, except for the Big Band CD Mike played. Several tunes were familiar from swing dances I'd attended, but the beat was infectious, and I wiggled in my seat in time to it.

"I like this music," Mike said. "It speaks to me. Sometimes I play classical numbers, but I always return to this era. It makes me feel alive."

We were sitting behind my house and I was sweating the next move. I didn't want him coming into my house. Definitely not a first date maneuver—out of the question.

"There's something about you, Mike, that fits you right into that era. It's as if you'd been plucked from the 40's and transplanted into the 2000's. It's as if you belong more in that time than this one." I didn't tell him about the crystal ball visions, for my gut feeling was to maintain secrecy for whatever reason.

"I'm a vintage sort of guy," he said. "Come on, I'll walk you to your door."

I felt glad our evening was ending, but also noticed a ball of anxiety in my mid regions. I hoped he wouldn't try to kiss me. One cup of hot chocolate didn't entitle him to a kiss.

We both stepped up on the back porch as my stomach clenched like a fist.

"You know, I've always wanted to see inside one of these," he began.

"Mike, I've had a nice evening, but it's getting late, so I'll just say good night."

"Really, a five minute tour will do it, then I'll be on my way." He stared over his glasses and in his deepest, sexiest voice said, "Please."

How does he do this, I wondered? How can he push the limits back so effortlessly?

"I'll show you the place, but just a few minutes. Then I'll have to say good night."

I saw the dog's face in the back door as it shook from her pounding on it.

"Is she going to bite me?" he asked as I unlocked the back door and swung it open.

"We'll test and see." I smiled brightly up at him, and then we headed in, me in the lead.

"Stay down, girl," I commanded as Princess barked at Mike. She leaped at me and managed to lick my face.

"I guess I passed inspection," he said as Princess sniffed him over. "It's hard to impress some dame if her dog doesn't like you."

"This is the kitchen which leads into the dining room," I said. He craned his neck as he took in the heavy dining room furniture and my decorating of the old home I already loved.

"This is nice, very nice." His face lit up. I could almost hear him calculating the real estate value of my property.

"And this is the living room. It's contemporary, but comfortable." I paused briefly. The cream, rose, and green couch and two green wing chairs were from my old place and not suited to the Victorian era. But for now they were comfortable and adequate.

"Are these original Victorian pieces or reproductions?" He pointed to my TV and DVD player.

I wrinkled my nose and said, "Yes, there was life before the DVD, but I can't remember it. I haven't really furnished the family room yet, around the corner, so if you'll follow me upstairs..." I motioned to the impressive dark wood carved stairway to the second floor. He started up and I followed.

"The bathroom," I pointed out, all light and mirror, yellow and green. I'd picked the colors of creativity and healing on purpose. He ducked his head in and grunted. I showed him the library, exercise room, and spare bedroom, and he glanced at them.

"Last, but a favorite room for me, the master bedroom. This is where I spend most of my time. I do some office work in here, too," I said, nodding toward my desk. I was suddenly aware of my crystal ball hidden beneath its black silk shroud on the bedside stand. I hoped Mike wouldn't notice it or touch it.

"This piece looks like it belongs with the house," he said, stepping over to the chest of drawers. I exhaled in relief.

89

"Yes, I got it at a local antique shop. It's just a reproduction, but it's fun, anyway."

I didn't like him in my bedroom, had chills tingling my spine, so I stepped out of the room and eased on into the hall. I think he knew my feelings, for he gave me a quizzical stare, then followed.

"You in some big hurry?" he asked, putting his arm around my shoulders.

"I think I told you I need to do some things before I go to bed. That five minute tour has expanded past fifteen minutes now. Please, I don't mean to sound cranky, but thank you for the evening."

He poked his head into the downstairs powder room and the stairs to the basement as if he didn't want to miss any feature.

"We didn't go out on the front porch. I love the big wrap-around porches on these places."

"Some other time. It's dark and there won't be much to see tonight. Of course, the porch is at its finest hour in the summer with hanging baskets of flowers, while you laze on the porch swing with a delicious little breeze soothing the body and the soul." I rattled on as I steered him back toward the kitchen.

"I brought a bottle of wine. It's in the truck," he said hopefully as a last resort.

"Thank you, Mike, but I really need to go." I opened the back door and leaned out. "Good night."

He leaned down and buzzed me on one cheek. "Next thing you'll be begging me not to leave. You dames are sure hard to figure." He tipped his hat, which he'd left on during the tour, and was gone into the dark.

I shut the door before the truck headlights lit the porch. I leaned back against the door as Princess brought Mr. Baseball Bat to me, poking him into my knees.

Mike had explored my house with more than the usual interest and had even pushed the issue to gain admittance to my place. Too intense, I thought, and too interested in the material end of my being. He seemed more interested in the house than in seducing me, the supreme insult; I smiled about it to myself. He was looking for a woman of property, but I was merely a woman with a high mortgage payment.

Or was he the man in my crystal vision, the one in the crowded room of swing dancers long ago? Did he remember? Had he been here before, and were these walls and rooms familiar to him?

I pulled my winter coat close around me, though I was inside, and felt very tired.

"I'm not sure if I want to see Mike again," I told Princess, who wisely blinked her brown eyes, then dropped her bat to lick my hand with great compassion.

Chapter Nine

"Brad, I thought we would begin today with the issue you raised at the end of your last session. Do you remember that?" I had been dying all week for the answers to my questions. He had intrigued me with his mysterious comment.

"Issue?" He looked blank, but still handsome in his black polo shirt and tan Dockers, shifting himself in the peach chair.

"You said something about your last relationship and compared it to your new one," I said hopefully.

"I don't remember," he said with a final tone.

"You said, 'I just hope it doesn't happen again.' You were referring to something in your past."

"Oh." His eyes looked blank. Or maybe guarded.

He talked about his car and about his work as a computer programmer. He talked at length and with great fervor, so that I could barely interject a comment. Finally, he paused.

"What about Janet? How is your budding relationship with her coming along?" I readjusted my black embroidered sweater over my white blouse and black skirt.

"Janet. I'm not sure about that. I need some time to think it over. I haven't seen her in the past week." His handsome face was inscrutable.

"Did you call her?"

"No."

"Did she call you?"

"She left a couple of messages on my answering machine. I didn't have time to call her back." He shifted again in the chair, and I knew he'd be happier talking about his job.

"You seemed happy with her last week. Of course beginnings are always when we shine brightest and best. Did some feelings about her surface?" I glanced at the perfect yellow rose on my desk, grateful for its presence, like a sunrise.

He looked down at his hands.

"Brad?"

He looked up quickly, his blue eyes blazing. "You don't understand, Dr. Westin. I don't think I can take a risk again. I can't let it happen again."

"Let what happen?" I tried to sound casual, but I was sitting on the edge of my office chair with my jaw clenched, and shaking him was beginning to sound like appropriate therapy.

"I nearly killed Danielle, the last girl I was with. If she hadn't been kind-hearted and loved me, I'd probably be in jail right now." His radiant eyes bored into me with misery and suffering.

"Oh, I see." But I didn't, not yet. Though I've listened to endless hours of stories and have trained myself to be detached, I occasionally register a shock. This was about 4.0 on the Richter scale.

When I had recovered sufficiently, I began to draw him out without any emotional display. He started to open up, now that the worst was out. I hadn't jumped up or run from the room or pointed a finger at him.

"You say you nearly killed Danielle. Can you tell me more about that?"

"I liked Danielle very much, and we were good friends as well as lovers. We had been together for about three months when the trouble began. She was so beautiful and strong and loving that I thought I would be all right this time."

"Tell me more about the trouble, Brad."

"Ever since I was a teenager I've had black moods. That's what my mother called them."

"Tell me more about your black moods."

"It was more than being in a bad mood or feeling out-of-sorts. I sometimes lapsed into rages, and I destroyed things—like the new bike my mom and dad bought me. I loved that bike."

"Did you ever hurt people?"

"Yes, I nearly broke my sister's arm one time. Her wrist was badly sprained. I know I never meant to hurt her."

"What about Danielle? What happened with Danielle?"

"We had been together for three months, like I said. We were going to bed one night and the next thing I knew she was thrashing about and my hands were around her neck. It was like I had just awakened from a nightmare." His expression, even now, showed amazement and disbelief.

"Was she badly hurt, Brad?" I asked gently, sensing his distress.

"Her neck was bruised and her voice was hoarse for a week. And of course that was the end of our relationship. So you can see why I'm reluctant to pursue a relationship with a woman."

"What triggers these rages, Brad? Can you tell me what happened or was said?"

"Nothing in particular. Some incident might get on my nerves, then the next thing I know I'm out of control. It's almost as if some other guy is doing these things."

"What about the incident with Danielle? Do you remember what happened there?"

He fingered a colorful glass paperweight on my desk. "I don't know," he said, crossing his legs and staring at the ceiling.

"Or maybe you don't want to think about it?" I didn't believe him for a minute.

He looked over and stared at me for a second. "I just don't know."

"I think we've made a lot of progress here today.

95

Unfortunately, our time is up for this session. We can address these issues again next week." Somehow, my little speech seemed dreadfully inadequate. My do-gooder instincts sometimes tripped me up, but I had to remember my limits, that I wasn't the Higher Power of my clients.

"Thanks, doctor. I need to get to the bottom of this mess. I'd really like to be normal, like the other guys."

"You find these normal guys and show them to me and then I'll believe they actually exist. And that goes for women, too," I said.

He grinned, and his face lit up. "Whoever your boyfriend is, he's one lucky guy. I've never met any woman like you in my travels. You're one special lady."

Brad took my hand and stared softly into my eyes. Suddenly lightheaded and more strongly attracted to him than ever, I slowly extricated my hand from his grasp.

"I thank you for the kind words, Brad. I'll see you next week at your regular session time."

This time he turned and walked away, closing my office door behind him with a little click. I stood up and leaned against my desk, holding both hands against my chest. My heart was thumping with abandon.

This one's getting complicated, though not unexpectedly so. I needed help. I pictured myself in quicksand up to my neck and knew struggling would only make it worse. I considered moving my office and changing my name at the least; for the first time, I wanted to sign off his case and send him away.

I could picture this handsome man with wings and a halo—Brad the angelic messenger, Mr. Perfect to the world's eyes. Yet beneath the exterior lurked demons, twisted and ugly, and I wondered if my methods could exorcise them.

Danger dwelled there, I could tell, and I reasoned that it was time to turn him over to another practitioner.

I had calmed now, breathing peacefully, and I knew I wouldn't do it. I'd continue with Brad as long as there was hope I could help him, whatever the price I'd pay later.

Crystal ball duty was at the top of my list at home that night. My successes had been sporadic. I'd hoped every session would add to my information, or that I'd have a breakthrough session when all the important scenes replayed. Not so, I'd discovered, for like life, I got whatever came next and not necessarily what I wanted.

The past week of scrying had been disappointing. I'd seen some lovely scenes: lovers surrounded by ocean on a tropical island, foreign pastoral locales with green rolling hills, other lifetimes in other places, but no 40's drama set here in Pittsburgh in my house.

I'd even tried four times a day for several days, but in the end, only clouds swirled through my crystal sphere. I felt so peaceful and hopeful gazing at the clouds, but the story lay in there, beyond the clouds, beyond my senses. This scrying was like viewing a television set without any way to switch the channels or to choose what I wanted and needed to watch.

I'd knocked off for the past few days, figuring I'd been trying too hard, so tonight could be the night. Yes, I had high hopes for the visions tonight, though my best bet was not to have any expectations.

Princess accompanied me to the bedroom and promptly fell asleep on the floor by my desk. We'd had a rousing romp in the park after work, during which she'd seemed to have forgotten all her telepathic commands. My mind was too squirrel-infested to send proper commands, anyway.

With her soft breathing as relaxation music, I did all my preparatory work and settled at my desk with the crystal ball. I contacted with the sphere almost immediately, and its energies flared up, especially alive tonight. A white fog rolled in, peppered with flecks of light.

The lights flashed like a prism of colors within, fascinating me as they circled and grew larger and brighter until the fog was obscured. Suddenly dazed, as if a camera flashed in my face, I became aware that I was inside a dance hall again. The place looked like the one where Jay had taken me for the swing dance, the same dance setting as before in the sphere. The crowd consisted of young men and women in 1940's attire gyrating to the Big Band sounds. I searched the crowd for the Mike look-alike, but didn't see him.

The band blasted away, and on the stage the seven men in white shirts and dark trousers belted out a fast tune. They played with their whole bodies, the two saxophone players continuing to wail it out with their eyes closed, as if they played eternally within this crystal sphere.

She stepped onto the stage from the wings, walking with great composure to the center, where a microphone awaited her. Her long, pink flowered dress swirled around her, the short sleeves and princess neckline accentuating her slim figure.

Flipping her flowing blonde hair behind her, she grasped the microphone in one hand. She smiled into the crowd and snapped the fingers of her free hand in time to the music as she swayed slightly and became dreamy-eyed.

She was the same blonde woman of my former vision, the one in the Victorian house just like mine.

And I still knew the woman was me. My gut feeling hadn't changed on that one.

She sang into the microphone, diving into the song at some prearranged beat. When she turned and flashed a smile at the band, they all waved back at her, so that the connection seemed intimate and good-natured.

I searched the faces of men and women not dancing and perceived respect as they listened to the woman. Their rapt interest proved they found her compelling, and her voice came through low, sexy, and mellow as she crooned a romantic number I'd never heard before.

She sang along with the band for three more numbers, then one of the saxophone players, a young man with slicked back hair, came forward, took the microphone, and announced the break. The crowd began to disperse.

The blonde singer looked into the crowd and her face lit up with recognition. She walked down a set of steps and at the bottom linked hands with a man who'd rushed up to greet her.

He grabbed her and delivered a bear hug that rocked her off her heels. His head balding and close-shaven, he lifted her up and turned, his face clearly in view.

He was the Mike guy, whatever his name was back in time, whoever he was to me, or to her then.

I longed to hear what they were saying to each other. She gestured with her hands and poked him in the side, and he nibbled on her neck. They linked arms and walked through a doorway, out of the scene, just as the fog rolled in.

No, I thought, as the scene faded. I need to know what happened next, what went on between these two. What does all this mean to me now?

Fluffy clouds filled the sphere again, and my tension turned to relief. There was more coming this time. I desperately needed to know more. My urgency gnawed at me.

The clouds cleared, and the hawk circled above the wooded area. The hawk soared in shadow, so blackened was he, but to my growing horror, I realized the bird was not a hawk, but a vulture—circling in lazy arcs, waiting.

Then I saw a body on the ground in the woods below—the blonde, her hair splayed out like a fan around her. The eyes were closed, arms crossed against chest, the body immobile on its back. Her purple dress flattered her, so that she resembled an elaborate doll, and I kept waiting for her to move.

"Get up," I said. "Hurry and get up."

But she didn't move, and her chest remained frightfully still. I looked closer at her, and noticed her skin, pale and blue-tinged, like marble.

Dead. She lay dead in the woods.

I shook myself. I lay dead in the woods.

Want more, I thought as the scene fogged over. This time when the mists faded, the crystal ball sat lifeless, clear with milky threads throughout it. I kept staring, horrified by the final scene. Now I knew my sense of urgency was justified. In the past, I had been killed or dumped dead in the woods, ending my life then as a young, vibrant woman.

Of course she was murdered, especially in light of Teddy's prophecy. But who? And how?

And why kill this lovely creature?

Princess placed her chin on my lap, and as I turned down to her, to the real world of the present moment, she gazed adoringly up at me. Her hair felt soft and steadying as I stroked her face and ears. The more I stroked, the more grounded I became. She sat sharing her doggy wisdom until the world of here and now returned, and I was able to get up again.

Chapter Ten

I' ve always remained friends with my former lovers, and in some ways John Gula was the big love of my life so far. Both originally from Pittsburgh, we'd lived together for several years during our psychology training at San Francisco State University. He'd been sweet, attentive, and a dynamo in the bedroom. I gave him even higher marks in lovemaking than he'd received on his dissertation.

Then, the bottom fell out and he abandoned me. I was never sure what happened, but on that bright spring day I rushed home early to make dinner, and John was treating another lady to sexual delights in our bed.

He couldn't tell me what went wrong, only that it no longer worked because I wasn't a tennis player (a sport he played as obsessively as his sexual pursuits). So he was both a great love and a bitter disappointment, the worst and best guy I ever dated.

Time has healed those wounds, and John and I stayed in touch. In the past six or seven years, we occasionally served as sounding boards for each other in difficult cases. It had been a few years since we'd talked, yet I knew I needed help handling Brad's case. When I'd called John, he'd been delighted to hear from me, and we arranged a meeting at his house the next day.

On this overcast, chilly afternoon, I followed his directions to Beaver, a river town north of Pittsburgh. I turned up a short hill and drove into an alley behind older homes to the small red brick house near a dirt turnaround. Somehow, the dead end seemed symbolic of our romantic relationship.

I pulled behind his black sports car and was getting out, testing some frozen mud with one shoe, when he appeared at the back door, a smile highlighting his face. He brushed his red-tinted dark brown hair out of his face and stood tall in pink short-sleeved shirt and cream slacks.

"Good to see you, Suzanne," he said, opening the door wide.

"It's nice of you to take me, doctor. After all, we doctors need to be doctored, too," I said, stepping into his kitchen.

"I can't think of a prettier head to examine than yours." He waved me through to his living room. "This might be a better place to work than in the computer room."

I stepped into what should have been the dining room to look at a computer on a desk filled with papers. An overwhelming amount of clutter—magazines, newspapers, and books—was tossed all around the desk and couch. The impression was utter chaos.

No, that hasn't changed. I knew that the same degree of clutter probably inhabited his basement and maybe the bedroom, too. I shuddered just thinking about it.

103

Could someone with all that untidiness throughout his house help bring order to my unquiet mind? Did the chaos of his living quarters correspond to chaos within his being? For an instant, I thought of excusing myself.

"Come have a seat here, Suzanne." John patted beside him on the striped orange and brown couch. A big television set, stereo system, and coffee table completed the room's furnishings. With white mini blinds instead of curtains and a hardwood floor, the look was stark, clinical, and lacking in creature comforts.

"Where do you do your therapy, John?" I said in amazement at his "office". I knew he worked at a pain management job at a local hospital, had studied business, and sometimes taught classes at a college.

"I haven't done much therapy lately, but I still take people here. I can't see laying out capital for an office right now. I've had some business dealings, done telephone work. I'm getting a free trip to the Bahamas out of it.

"So, shall we begin?" he said. "Your call surprised me, since it's been so long. It's always good to hear from a former classmate."

"Funny that we had to travel from here to San Francisco to meet, but I would hardly call us classmates. We were more than that," I said, then wished I hadn't.

"You interested in a reunion? Just for you and me?"

"Maybe I shouldn't have come," I looked for the escape route from the room. I'm a flighter, not a fighter.

"I'm just teasing," he said. But he wasn't, I could tell. "You had concerns you wanted to bounce off me. Let's work on that right now. You said something about a male client."

"Yes, his name is Brad. Right from the beginning I found myself sexually attracted to him."

"What are you telling me this for?" His face tensed and a vein throbbed in his neck.

"I thought as a fellow psychologist you could give me some insight into the situation. Would you feel more comfortable if I didn't talk about him?"

"Did you have sex with him?" His eyes narrowed.

"Of course not. He's a client." I yanked my teal sweater down over my jeans.

"All right, then, I understand about the attraction thing. Feel free to unload on me, Suzanne." He wiggled over closer to me on the couch until our thighs were snuggled together.

"You sure?" Was I more amused or annoyed at his nearness? Since I needed his help with the Brad dilemma, I decided to ignore it.

"Very sure. You're here. I'm a psychologist, you're a psychologist. So let's get to the bottom of your client situation."

"So, like I said, this Brad I found attractive, and he comes to me for therapy because he says he can't do relationships with women."

"Tell me about it," John said, his eyes rolling up.

105

"I know. Me, too, only men instead. So, I thought I could help him, but it's more complicated than it looked. He has a history of rages, and he choked his last girlfriend, hurt her badly."

"Geez."

"And at the end of this session, he started turning the charm on me. It was very distracting, especially since I felt attracted to him initially." I wondered if John thought I was overreacting to the situation.

"How do you feel about his attraction to you?"

"I didn't feel much one way or the other. I guess I am a psychologist first and foremost, even though I've had silly feelings for him. I don't think it's going to be a problem. Funny, I hadn't figured that out on my own."

"You're too close to it."

And you're a little too close for comfort. I inched away from him till our legs barely touched. "I think when I heard about his rages and his behavior with Danielle, the girlfriend, my feelings toward him changed."

"Is there something else about this situation that is bothering you?" He glanced down at our leg connection.

"I have a feeling of unease about doing therapy with him now. I can't quite pinpoint it, though." This living room was quiet, with no road noise or outside voices, and I was relaxing in spite of our leg mating.

"You say he is coming on to you and that he was violent with his last girlfriend. Does that say anything to you?" He looked at me searchingly as I turned the situation over in my mind.

"That's it, then. If he sees me as a sex object or as a desirable woman, I could be in physical danger from him."

"Exactly. And I think the threat might be real, not just our overactive imaginations. How will you handle this situation? I hope you do take action on this one, since I like having you as a friend." He squeezed my hand, which would have sent my pulses racing in the old days. How lovely that some things do change.

"I can talk with him at the beginning of our next session and make it perfectly clear that ours is a therapist-client relationship. I'll make him understand that I am a therapist, not a female or a prospective girlfriend."

"You look like a female to me." He waggled his eyebrows.

"You're not my client. So I'll be alert to any more advances on his part. If he continues that behavior, I will terminate as his therapist. I can send him to you, John." I smiled sweetly.

"Thanks a lot, but I'll pass on that one. He'd probably get mad and set my house on fire."

"It's brick."

"You know what I mean."

We discussed the Brad situation a few more minutes, and then I remembered my entire unwritten agenda for our meeting. "There's something else bothering me."

"You want to go upstairs and relive the good old days when we went to bed and barely slept?"

"You know my position on that." I wiggled over so our thighs were free again.

"Position. You're thinking about positions. You can leave the driving to me." He grabbed my hand and started to stand up.

"I just have one more concern," I said, yanking him back down on the couch. "Are you ready to listen? And I do appreciate your assistance."

He nodded his head and settled down beside me.

"I've been using a crystal ball to get in touch with my past lives."

"Scrying. What did you see?" A sudden spark in his hazel eyes alerted me to his interest.

"I've been transported back in time to the Big Band era, and I see a blonde woman living in a Victorian house like mine. She's a singer with a band, and I've seen a man at the dance with her."

"What does that have to do with you? Other than the house, I mean."

"I always get a strong feeling that the woman is—I should say was—me. Me in a former lifetime."

"Anything specific about the man?"

"They seem to love each other. I went to the swing dance in Pittsburgh and met a man who looks exactly like him. And another thing, I bought an antique dresser locally, and it was in the past life, too."

He fingered his chin. "It's interesting, but why would any of this be a problem?"

"The last time I gazed, I saw the blonde woman on the ground in the woods somewhere. She looked pretty dead."

"Not natural causes?"

"Very unnatural. And before that a friend on the other side warned me of trouble coming my way. He said if I didn't figure it out, I could be murdered. He said it was a pattern that went back for lifetimes for me.

"So I wonder, John, if I'm in some kind of danger, if someone will try to kill me."

John held up one finger and excused himself, and after several minutes, I became aware of a spicy aroma in the air. He returned with two aromatic mugs of chai tea latte. "What friend on the other side? You mean the spiritual plane of existence? Someone who's dead?"

I nodded my head. "Scrying can sometimes produce the appearance of dead loved ones. Remember the work of Dr. Raymond Moody? This friend was a man I dated a few months right before he died."

"He appeared to you and told you this stuff?" he asked, his face puzzled.

I nodded solemnly, sipping the delicious brew.

"If it were me, I'd do a hypnotic regression to reinforce this information and get more. Scrying is all well and good, but there's nothing like hypnosis to get to the root of things."

"I agree. Will you regress me?"

"Sure thing. Maybe a day on the weekend. I'll come over to your place if you want."

I stood and stretched. "I feel better already. What do I owe you for the session today?"

"The usual—you can reciprocate when I'm down and out. That could be any moment now."

"I'll fix you dinner. How about Saturday night around seven?"

"Great. I haven't done a regression in a while. It'll be fun."

When I heard the knock at the back door, with Princess barking and jumping on it, I consulted my watch. Five thirty—too early for it to be John. I was setting the dining room table and getting ready to make a salad.

I stepped into the kitchen and spied the familiar shape through the lace curtain. I hadn't seen him in quite a while.

"James, I've missed you," I said and swung wide the kitchen door, revealing his grinning face.

"I've been ever so far away," he said, pointing to his house next door. "I hadn't heard from you for so long, thought I'd better check on you two."

He came inside, then roughhoused with Princess on the floor. As he stood up, he stared at the place settings on the table and cleared his throat. "Am I interrupting something?"

"I'll have to get back to work in a few minutes. I invited a friend to dinner."

"That bald guy with the red truck?"

"James! Have you been spying on me?" I couldn't help but be amused, but tried to sound stern.

"I just notice things." His face became blank, unreadable.

"I shouldn't tell you, because you're acting silly, but he's a fellow psychologist. He's been helping me with some of my issues and he's not the bald guy. He has hair."

James raised his eyebrows as if he knew all about my issues. "I just came over to see if you wanted to walk Princess, but I guess you're too busy right now getting ready for a romantic dinner."

"Not romantic and probably only barely edible. But I promised him dinner, so no dog walk tonight for me. But thank you for asking."

"She won't get her walk tonight, then?"

"I just don't have time. She rarely misses a walk." Princess was standing between us, head turning from James to me as we intoned the magical word, "walk."

His face grew alert. "I'll take her."

"You sure?" I hated to take advantage of his good nature.

"Of course, I'll take her. I'll bring her back later."

"If I don't answer the door, we may be in the middle of a therapy session. You can just pop Princess in the back door. I'll leave it open."

"Therapy, huh?" He sounded skeptical.

"James, what is wrong with you tonight? If I didn't know better, I'd say you were getting jealous. That's not like you at all."

"Don't worry, Suzanne, I'm not fruiting out on you. It doesn't mean anything. I'll just take Princess for a walk, keep her over at my house for a while, then bring her by later."

"Thanks, amigo. She might give you one of her rawhide bones for this."

James grabbed the leash off the wall hanger. Princess perked up and rushed over to him, allowing him to snap it to her collar. She threw a couple of worried glances at me.

"It's all right, girl. James is going to take you for a walk. Go ahead. See you later, girl."

She wasn't sure about going without me, but once they were out the kitchen door, she was frisking along beside him.

The house echoed with extreme quiet when she was gone. Her constant companionship was something I treasured even more than this house and its comforts. I could overlook chewed socks and tufts of dog hair everywhere when I realized her true value, her devotion and care.

I ran upstairs, changed clothes, patted my hair, and then finished my kitchen work. The salad was on the table, the spaghetti nearly cooked when I heard another knock. John was beaming at me when I opened the door.

"Dr. Gula, I presume?"

"Dr. Westin, you look lovely tonight. Turn around so I can see you. Pink—my favorite color." He stepped inside and twirled me under one arm. I'd worn a cream silky blouse and a long mauve print skirt that lifted up and out.

"You look pretty nice yourself," I said, not wanting to sound too enthusiastic since I'd sworn long ago to never get involved with him again. He did look charming in his pink shirt and cream slacks that he wore frequently, almost like a uniform. Enhanced by his endearing smile.

Sometimes he looked so attractive that I weakened and questioned my vow, but he had been the most disastrous love affair of all time. When vulnerable, I reminded myself of that.

"It's ready, John. Are you hungry?"

"An hour spent with Suzanne is like a week at the Bahamas. At the Atlantis resort. Yes, I'm hungry. It smells great in here."

"I thought we could eat first, then I could show you around if you want, then we could do the regression." I put some Big Band music on the stereo system, since I knew John liked it, too. A jazzy tune filled the room, and I broke into a hearty rock step.

"Now, that's music," he said, swinging me into an open space between the table and a big window. We danced the entire number before we broke apart, laughing.

113

"I didn't know you were a swing dancer. You're quite good. You lead with authority and style," I said, just a little out of breath.

"I didn't know you were a swing dancer, either. So we've independently developed the same skill, another indication that we belong together." He said the last as I slid into the kitchen to check on dinner.

"It just means swing is popular right now. I'm bringing out the food."

"Need help?"

"Just with the eating end of it." I appeared with two plates of spaghetti.

Our conversation flowed gently throughout dinner. John declined his second glass of wine because he desired his "hypnotic powers to be unimpaired."

"That reminds me," I said as we finished and both stood up. "You aren't going to try anything this time, are you?"

"Try what?" His face blanked out.

"Last time you tried to use post hypnotic suggestion to get me into bed."

"I don't remember that." A sheepish grin belied his words. "What a great idea, though."

"Promise not to do that?"

"I promise." I noticed his fingers crossed behind his back.

I toured him around the house, and he exclaimed his approval in each room. Finally, in the bedroom, he asked that all important question: "Where shall we set up for your regression, Suzanne?"

I hadn't even thought of that. I deliberated briefly, then said, "Those two wing chairs in the living room might work. What do you think?"

He nodded, and we trooped back downstairs just as I heard knocking at the back door.

"Anybody home?" James called from inside the door as Princess strained at the leash. He unhooked her, and mayhem and confusion reigned for several minutes.

Princess ran right to John, whose arms were locked at his sides, his eyes wide with fear. She jumped up on him, barking. James hid an evil grin behind one hand and choked on his laughter.

I grabbed Princess by the collar, pulled her down, and commanded her to sit. She tried to leap on the hapless Dr. Gula again, so I shoved her toward the cellar and down a few steps, shutting the door in her surprised face.

"Sorry, John." I dusted off his pink shirt front. "I forgot you were afraid of dogs."

"She's a bit overwhelming," he said, beginning to recover from the trauma.

"John, this is our neighbor, James Rummel. He kindly offered to walk the dog for me tonight. James, this is John Gula, my psychologist friend who has come over to shrink a fellow shrink's head."

They nodded, shook hands and mumbled pleasantries, but the tension in the room could have generated electricity. I waited for the bell to ring so they could come out of their corners fighting.

"I can see you're busy, Suzanne. I just wanted to bring Princess home to you. She was most playful tonight." James nodded and backed out the door, which he shut so soundly that the wall vibrated. Gentle whimpers flowed around and through the basement door.

"I'm ready, Suzanne," John said stiffly.

"I know that was unpleasant. Had we better try again some other day?" I held my breath, hoping he wouldn't take me up on it.

He smiled and appeared to be loosening up. "No, now will be fine. Let's gravitate to the living room and send you back to your past. Just one thing, though."

"What's that?"

"You'll keep the dog cooped up, won't you?"

Chapter Eleven

"*Y*ou ready?" John asked, composed and sitting comfortably in the green wing chair. We had carefully positioned the chairs face to face. I'd lit two deep pink candles on the nearby coffee table, their scent sweet and relaxing, and dimmed the lights.

"Absolutely. I'm in your hands."

"I'm going to let that one go. Now, I want you to close your eyes and listen to my voice. Just follow me and I'll take you back to another place, another time. Keep in mind, Suzanne, that we are seeking a piece of the puzzle. We're looking for a past lifetime that relates to the present, to a possible threat on your life. With a little bit of luck, that'll surface, anyway.

"The present and these past lives are all connected and one in the continuum that is your eternal soul, your essence. So follow me as we walk on a beach at night. The moon is bright and full, and you can hear the waves crashing on the shore.

"You walk until you come to a temple made of marble illuminated by lights. It looks familiar, set up on a rocky bluff. Your feet take a path from the shore to the temple, and before

117

you know it you're there. Walking up five steps, you enter a beautiful sacred place with huge, green plants and fountains spraying up exuberantly. All is filled with light and a feeling of peace.

"You look straight ahead and see an archway that says 'Library of the Past.' Inside are books on shelves on all four walls. You pull a large green and gold volume down. Across the front of it is written 'Suzanne Westin.' There are other names below that, but you are unable to read them. You open the book and point a finger at a page.

"This is the lifetime you will visit. Put the book away and go to the back wall of the library where there is a green and gold door with symbols carved on it. Stand before the door as you are carried into a deeper and deeper state of relaxation.

"As I count down from ten to zero, you will feel more relaxed. Ten, nine, eight..., one, zero.

"You push on the door and it opens out, swings easily. You step a foot out and you look around. You have stepped into a past lifetime that relates to your present day problems."

As John talked me through, I was aware of his voice, his direction, but also cognizant of the story unfolding before me. It seemed real to me, as if I were really there, and as the scenes unfolded, I was living them—again.

"Where are you?" he asked.

"London, England."

"What year is it?"

"1803."

"What are you wearing?"

"I'm wearing striped trousers and a white shirt, starched at the collar, and a tie, and a black jacket and black bowler hat."

He hesitated. "What's your name?"

"Gerald Smith."

"Have you a story to tell us, something we need to know to help Suzanne with her present uncertainties?"

I could hear myself talking to John, and the words flowed easily. "I am a musician and play the piano with considerable talent. I play in clubs throughout London, sometimes at private parties of the gentry. I love performing, I love the adulation I sometimes get, and I love mixing with the landed, wealthy class, though my class is a bit below that.

"Last year in my travels I came upon a beautiful young woman smitten with me. She was a singer with a voice sweet and haunting. She added tremendously to my act with quaint ballads and heart-wrenching tunes. She gladly joined me in my work.

"Heart-wrenching—now there's an apt description. This woman who was such an easy conquest, who tripped willingly to my bed and favored me with her womanly charms, just as easily flew away from me. For after three months of our affair, our collusion in song, she began to fail me. At first she said, 'Gerry, I'm tiring of this life. I think it's not for me.'"

I heard myself laughing, but not from mirth—a low, dry chuckle. "And I the one who never gave his heart, who did not

119

mingle love and business. What a pathetic chap I had become, clinging to her, begging her to stay.

"'Gerry, I think I must go,' she said. How I wish now I had let her go, banished her from my thoughts. For within a fortnight, I returned home early from a solo engagement to find she'd welcomed another man into our bed." I stopped and sniffled slightly.

"What happened then?" John asked, his voice steady.

"There was a great lot of confusion and the man slipped out our bedroom window. She stayed to face the music. Appropriate for a singer, yes? She assumed her perfect little body and angelic face would win me back to her, but she never counted on blind rage.

"For I had loved her and she had utterly betrayed me. I grabbed her and shook her and shook her until she learned her lesson. I called to her on the ground, but she was pale and still. I realized my hands had been around her throat and that I'd choked the life from her.

"I held her to me tenderly, but there was no breath in her body. So I cried over her and wished that I had never met her. She had seduced me, made me love her, then betrayed me. It wasn't fair."

"What is happening to you now, Gerry?" John said. "What was the consequence of your actions?"

"Oh, they'll hang me soon. I don't suppose there's any way out of that. All for my folly, because I gave my heart to a woman. Women are most malicious creatures."

"Suzanne, it's time to come back now from this past life. I am going to count slowly from zero to ten. Please follow me and return to here and now. But please first remember all that you have said."

I heard him counting up and slowly returned to the room. By the time he had reached ten, I was opening my eyes.

"That was very interesting," John said, standing up and stretching. He sat back down and looked at me. "What do you make of all this? Does this shed light on what you were hoping to find out?"

I stretched, too. How strange that I had gone far, far away. "It's all fascinating, but we skipped way back to 1803 instead of the Big Band era. This wasn't the story I'd hoped to relive."

"But it's all related, all a piece in the puzzle. Maybe it's a recurring pattern. You have to get inside the pattern to break it. Evidently, you're doing that this lifetime."

"But what does Gerald Smith have to do with me, the blonde in the Big Band era? I don't see the connection."

"When you have more information, you will. You already have seen her lying lifeless in the woods, most probably murdered. But in England you were the man who murdered in a jealous rage, not the one murdered."

"Fascinating," I said, a shiver tracing up my spine. "Why can't there be stories about someone winning prizes, being wealthy and living the good life? Why did I get a story about betrayal and murder?"

121

John smiled. "You know that yourself. You may be in danger—in fact, it's highly likely. This is all a warning for you. How lucky to be warned."

"Funny, I don't feel lucky." I blinked my eyes and looked around the room to help ground me back to the here and now.

"Shall I comfort you with carnal acts in case the end is near?"

"Oh, now you're making fun of me. How can I believe in any of this?"

"I'm sorry, Suzanne, but when I'm near you..."

"So maybe you're the killer, John."

"You ought to suspect everyone and anyone," he said, suddenly serious. "But don't think it's me. I just want to use you and cast you aside, then use you some more."

"I really do appreciate your help, my friend. I thank you for this evening. I guess it's time to call it a night."

We rose and exchanged more pleasantries, but before he went he offered his services in the future, if needed.

"I thank you, John," I said as he headed out through the kitchen. "You never know when you might need a good man."

Though I was relaxed from being hypnotized, I felt that little twist in my belly that had become so familiar to me. I was disappointed with the information I'd received, and time would soon run out. Upstairs, in the bedroom, I lifted the crystal ball to my cheek. The buzzing felt warm and fuzzy, and I knew the answers lay waiting inside. I wished that I had the energy to scry tonight, but exhaustion had swamped me. I vowed to keep up with my efforts, to try again as soon as possible

Tomorrow. I'll scry and discover the answers tomorrow.

As I drifted toward the gentle seas of sleep, thoughts yet passed through my mind, some truths my waking self had not yet connected:

John brought another woman into our bed when we lived together. In 1803, it happened to Gerald Smith—me, again. What in the world could that mean?

Chapter Twelve

"*H* old still. This is for your own good."

Pinned down, Princess struggled to escape as I clipped fur balls from her long, shaggy fur. I tried to keep her brushed, but knots formed anyway and would eventually mat her coat. I made one last careful clip close to her skin as the phone began ringing.

"Saved by the ringer, puppy girl," I said, waving the scissors one last time before tossing them down. The sun beamed rainbows onto the bedroom walls from two faceted crystal ornaments hanging in the windows. I lifted the bedside phone.

"Am I interrupting anything important? Have you been predicting the future for your clients with your crystal ball? You know, I was there when it all began." Sandy's voice, as always, cheered me.

Sandy and I gabbed at length about family and friends, and then she asked again about the gazing. "Did you really scry and find out anything?"

I hesitated a second only, for this was Sandy. I'd been confiding in her for years.

"Some strange stuff has come up. I scry and see the Big Band era and people swing dancing and a guy asks me to dance. Then I go to a swing dance here in Pittsburgh, and the *same guy* is there and asks me to dance."

A long, long pause—longer than she has ever paused before.

"You there, Sandy?"

"That's almost creepy, Suz. Is this a joke?"

"No. No joke. I went out with him. To find out what it was all about."

"Maybe you should be careful. It's so weird. How was he?"

"He seemed all right, maybe a little too interested in my real estate."

"*He's been to your house?*" Sandy's voice raised an octave as her inevitable mothering instincts kicked in. "Right away?"

"Don't worry. I'm a big girl." I couldn't help but smile, although her anxiety was infectious.

"Jonathon! He's going to baptize the cat with a cup of water. Call you later."

A few minutes later, the phone rang again, so I picked up and said, "Did you catch him in time, before the cat got it?"

Another pause, and then, "Suzanne?"

"Mike?"

"Catch who in time?"

"Never mind. Guess you aren't Sandy calling me back. Sorry."

125

He cleared his throat. "Should I hang up so this other, inferior guy can call you back?"

"My girlfriend's four-year-old was about to give their cat a bath, so she hung up." I hoped my words weren't tainted by my amusement at his male suspicious nature.

"Oh. You can't blame me, you being such a gorgeous dame and all. What's been happening, anyway?"

We conversed for twenty minutes. I learned a man who talks on the phone for a living is good at telephone conversations. There were no awkward moments, and our flowing discourse endeared him to me, in spite of his frequent relapses into pure bull.

During our talk, though, I kept waiting for him to get to the point and wondering what my response would be. I wasn't sure if I wanted to go out with him again. So when he calmly slipped it into a quiet ebb in the talk, when I least expected it, my defenses were down.

"Hey, Suzanne, I enjoyed our coffee date. Have you seen the new movie at the Rex?"

"No, I haven't. Is it something good? I don't get to the movies often."

"It's an Italian movie with English subtitles. Supposed to be very charming and uplifting. Want to go Saturday night?"

How could I tell the man that he'd been in my crystal ball vision? Suddenly, intuition alerted me, that if I got to know this Mike, I might learn more about my past, too. My fear was overshadowed by curiosity.

"That would be great," I heard myself saying before I could reconsider. A tightness at my throat prevented me from saying any more.

"Should I pick you up at your place?" he asked.

My throat thawed long enough for me to say, "Not necessary. I'll just meet you over there. What time does the movie start?"

"7:30. Meet you in front at 7:15. That way we'll get good seats. Then maybe we can go somewhere afterwards for dessert or coffee or herbal tea, whatever."

"That'll be great. Thanks for calling, Mike."

"Okay, doll. We could go dancing somewhere if you want, but you don't seem as big on it as I am."

"The movie sounds great. I'll see you at 7:15."

So, movie and dessert. We hadn't graduated to dinner, yet, but things were escalating, anyway.

Strangely, I felt happy about seeing Mike again. I hugged myself in the stillness of my bedroom to try plugging into my deeper emotions. Yes, it was definitely all right. For now, I sensed that I had nothing to fear from him.

I got ready for work, trying to keep the visions out of my mind, the pictures I 'd witnessed in the crystal ball—pictures of Mike and the blonde singer, the scene of the blonde me in the woods prostrate, not moving, not even breathing.

I shut it all out and hugged Miss Princess, kissing her shaggy head as she sulked. I stepped out back and connected with another pristine fall day, and looked forward to hearing about others' problems as a means of forgetting about my own.

"You were telling me about Janet?" I said to Brad, who was sitting in the peach chair beside my desk. His gaze had wandered to the one window in my office, as if the world outside was more interesting than the world inside him. He was easily distracted, vague, and distant today.

"Janet?" His gaze showed surprise, puzzlement, and then as reality sank in, engagement. "Were we talking about Janet? I'm having trouble focusing today."

"I asked if you were still seeing her. You were pretty taken with her in the beginning, and I was happy for you."

"Janet. Yes, I liked her. I couldn't call her for the longest while, and I didn't return her calls. After my terrible ending with Danielle, I wasn't sure if I wanted to try it again."

"How did your dating Janet begin? Where did you meet her?"

"I met her at a party. I almost didn't go that day. I went with another guy, a friend of a friend.

"I noticed Janet right away. She has striking good looks—dark, long hair and fine features. She stands out from the crowd. So I began talking to her, and the conversation was light and fun. I felt completely at ease with her.

"The next thing I knew, I was asking for her phone number. That went smoothly, too. Getting together with her went quite well. If only I didn't have this problem. Janet's a great person."

"So is anything going on between you two now? What's your current status?"

"I called her a couple of times and we set up a date. I was supposed to meet her at a movie. I tried to go. I got dressed and drove in the right direction, but I stopped at a bar first." He turned toward me without making eye contact.

"And?"

"I never went to the movie. That's a terrible thing to do to her, I know. She didn't call me. I guess she's had it with me. And I didn't have the nerve to contact her again.

"So I guess it's off between Janet and me." He'd squeezed his keys in one fist, his jaw tightening.

"What about calling her and asking to talk over your feelings? You could even talk about it over the phone so she wouldn't risk being stood up again." I didn't want to feel sorry for him, but even a therapist is a person at heart.

"I've thought of that. It's just so hard to get back into a relationship once things get off track. Most of this is because of my scene with Danielle."

"You mean when you flew into a rage and tried to choke her?" This seemed to be an important scene in his history. I scooted out a little on my chair, leaning forward.

"I was choking her. How can I tell Janet about that? How can I tell her I tried to strangle my last girlfriend? Do you think she'd still see me then?" His voice raised only a few notches, but his face contorted with emotion, so that he appeared handsome and tormented at the same time, like the leading man in some movie.

"You never know, Brad. You never can predict the opinions and behavior of others. She might fool you. Even if she told you to hit the road, you'd be right where you are now, anyway." I was fingering a smoky quartz crystal I'd brought from home. It was supposed to ground and protect me from negative forces, and I wasn't taking any chances.

"I might call her. I don't think she'll want to hear from me again."

"Backtracking a little, I don't think I remember what happened that day when you and Danielle staged the final scene—the choking episode. Can you fill me in on what happened and what triggered the rage?" *Come on, Brad.*

"I don't know."

"What do you mean?"

"I've thought it over many times, doctor. It's all blank. I can't remember much at all. I went over to Danielle's apartment, and we were both in a good mood. She made us dinner; we had chicken and broccoli and baked potatoes. She put a movie on the DVR, and that's it. The rest is blank until I woke up choking her."

"Did you ask her what happened?"

"She didn't want to talk to me after that," he said and examined his fingernails.

"Do you think you could ask her now?"

130

"She hangs up when I call her. The last time I tried, a man answered. I decided not to call her anymore."

"I see our time is nearly up for today, Brad. Is there anything else you wanted to talk about before we end for today?"

"I've been thinking about how nice you are to me, Suzanne." He choked slightly on the words.

"That's part of the job. If I weren't nice, all my clients would go somewhere else." Prickles of alarm raised on my back.

"I was just wondering if you were married or anything."

"No, I'm not married. Why do you ask, Brad?" A little stab of pain shot through my hand from squeezing the crystal.

"You seem to understand me, Doc. I really like you, too. I was wondering if we could get together some night for a drink."

Whoa! What is this? The client I had been attracted to initially was asking me out. Not only that, this was the guy who had nearly strangled his former girlfriend. Seeking reassurance of my acceptance of him?

"Thank you for asking, Brad. You're a very nice man and I like you, but I don't ever socialize with clients. The moment I would start seeing you on a friendly basis, I'd be no good to you as a therapist. That's the beauty of therapy—professional distance. From a distance I'm able to help my clients with their problems and not become a part of the problem."

131

"I don't think having a drink together would be that big of a deal," he persisted. He radiated charm, everything about him appealing at that moment.

"I would have to sign off your case first and you would no longer be a client."

"Well, we could do that."

"Unfortunately, I've just begun dating someone, so that wouldn't work for me. Besides, I like working with you as your therapist. I'd rather not pursue this any further," I said, not at all flattered by his attention, merely tense and on guard.

"I see," he said as if he didn't.

"I'll be glad to continue as your therapist, Brad. If that doesn't work for you, I could help you find another counselor."

"No, no, no. I guess I'm not thinking straight about all this. The male-female thing can be mighty powerful, yet confusing."

"You've said a lot. But since I'm helping you with your relationships with women, I can't become a part of the problem. I won't."

"Okay, Suzanne," he said, standing up. "I'll get it straight in my head. I won't mention it again. I just need to work on my problems. You've been a big help."

I smiled and waved and looked wise and therapeutic-like as he departed. I only had five minutes until the next client.

I suddenly realized my knees were quivering.

I smiled in relief and talked out loud, a healing, therapeutic method for me. "A few minutes of deep breathing

132

might be in order here. And Suzanne, dear, you've got to get another job."

Chapter Thirteen

*H*ome beckoned to me that night as I returned from the office and my altercation with Brad. The Victorian reposed majestically on the hill beside James's twin house, and I savored the beauty of the intricate architecture. The teal and rose trim cheered me, the beige soothed me, and as I exited the car, I knew more enjoyment lay in store for me.

Princess stood in the middle of the kitchen, her tail flailing wildly, so that she looked like a room cooling device. This was our ritual, for she was always waiting and never failed to give me a greeting that even a dignitary or celebrity would envy.

Little yelps of endearment and licks on my face rounded out the royal greeting as I knelt down to hug her. I was still both agitated and extremely weary from my session with Brad, yet at this moment Princess's coat felt comforting on my hands. I treasured this gentle, loving creature, my constant companion here in the manse.

I stood up and stretched. Home brought me home to myself. I smelled the two red roses on the dining room table, and the tiny whiff of sweetness quieted me. All around me, I received solace from the home I had decorated, in the soft lights, bright colors, and gleam of shining glass and wood.

Though I'd deposited paperwork from my practice on the dining room table, the laundry was heaped high, and some nearly overdue bills lay waiting upstairs, I knew my mission for the evening. The conflict with Brad had strengthened my resolve to take control of my life. Maybe tonight I'd celebrate a big breakthrough, and my life would be given back to me.

I walked Princess briefly, for the cold night wind bit its way through my black down coat. Her fur blew every way except off, but she didn't seem to mind as long as her pack leader led the way.

We landed back home in the dining room with me crunching a salad and her gnawing a new rawhide bone. I mentally rehearsed my game plan for the evening, trying to visualize a successful session. Part of me reasoned that I was too exhausted to scry, but the greater voice shouted that I had no choice but to try. Though most sessions still weren't productive, I expected that the more I exerted myself, the sooner the right vision would materialize.

We raced up the stairs to the bedroom. The room represented perfect order, furniture shining, bed made, all clutter conquered. I could have been a princess in her turret room, and the calming surroundings relaxed me even more. Here was my solitude, my peace.

Though my body yearned to collapse on the bed, I scanned beyond it until the black silk scarf caught my eye. I

135

pulled off the silky material, and rainbows within the crystal greeted me, and my connection reignited with this sphere. Holding it to my chest, I closed my eyes, once again sensing its energy coursing throughout me. The waves of energy shot upward and downward; at the same time, my hands and arms buzzed clear up into my jaws and head. It always excited and mystified me.

Such power, I wondered, gazing into the sphere again, resonating with it. I would have been drawn to this stone, even if I hadn't had a mission to accomplish. How I wished that I was looking for something less urgent—maybe a romantic partner, a past life as a duchess, or a new pathway for my career.

I readied the room for scrying, lit the candle, and settled back on the bed with the black silk beneath the ball. Within a few minutes of deep breathing and relaxing into the comfort of the bed, my entire body softened. My mind cleared, its chatter fading away. I prayed that it would be simple this time, a nice, easy regression to my former self.

As if in answer, light flickered within the ball, clouds with rays of light shooting through like a sunrise. It portended a new beginning for me, or perhaps a past long forgotten, some existence foggy now, like last night's dream.

The images came forth quickly now, and I became absorbed in them immediately.

The blonde woman was back, alive, so the story had to be out of sequence. She showed up again in this house, but not really this house—that long ago one that barely resembled mine on the interior. I didn't want to believe that she was me, yet I felt it stronger than ever now.

I tried not to think too hard about it.

The blonde sat at the dining room table with a man who was small and balding, with short gray-brown hair and glasses. As they ate, the girl talked animatedly. She jumped up suddenly, continuing to talk, massaging his neck and shoulders.

He turned, reaching for her hand, pulling her around onto his lap, kissing her. Next he was tugging at her red dress, his hands moving over her body. This guy was not the Mike twin, but another man with a cunning face.

She stood up, heaved a deep breath, picked lint off his olive business suit, and readjusted his flashy gold and red tie. A diamond glinted off his one hand, another flashed from a tie bar.

They continued to talk, and then she reached down and grabbed his hand, the one with the big diamond ring. She pulled him up, her face excited, a big, slow smile spreading across his weasel face.

Since I didn't hear anything this time, it was like watching a silent movie. I grew increasingly uneasy.

She was taller than he was, even in her bare feet, not that it mattered. He slid his arm around her waist, hers around his shoulders, and they walked toward the stairs. As they started up, I felt sick, as if some great injustice had been done, though I didn't know who he was or especially who he was to her. I hoped the crystal vision wouldn't accompany them to the bedroom, yet I couldn't stop watching. The tense moments passed like hours.

Gratefully, the scene faded to clouds, and then to a field of flowers. The sun shone down with the golden rays of late afternoon, a breeze tossing the tall grasses and flowers of purple, blue, orange, and yellow. I could feel the same breezes on my face, in my hair. Butterflies danced amidst the foliage, and peace pervaded the scene.

Peace. After the preceding vignette with the mystery man, this portrait of earth's bounty renewed me. A lazy afternoon, nodding blooming plants, other meadow creatures living in the foliage—I almost forgot about Mr. Weasel. But not quite.

"Princess," I said, sinking to the floor, snuggling up to her, "this story is beginning to stink. There's something rotten about all this. The woman seemed genuinely happy with the Mike guy. And now this little shifty guy has somehow come into focus in an intimate role. He's not even her type. It doesn't make sense, not one iota of sense."

Princess gently laid her chin on my leg, looking up with those soulful brown eyes, eyes that knew and forgave all. I had never before encountered such blind trust and unconditional love.

"I didn't have you with me in that lifetime, girl. That's where I went wrong. Now I have a guardian angel dog to keep me safe. Things will be different this time around. They will."

She thumped her tail in appreciation of my kind words. I tried to swallow, but a knot like a clenched fist in my throat made it difficult.

These stories would have been fascinating if they had been about someone else—no professional distance here. It had all become real and so deadly.

I held a hand to my throat to ease my tension. I was making progress and learning about my unfortunate past, and feeling sorry for her, whatever she did, whoever she was. Even without our past life connection, I connected with this exotic flower who pursued her own will.

More awake now, I stared around the bedroom with new eyes, wondering what the walls could tell me, how many sobs and cries they had absorbed. What scenes transpired in this room back in time? Yes, I was the blonde singer back in the 40's, and my life was even more frustrating and out of control then, even sordid, I feared.

I steered a little recklessly toward town and exited off the parkway, not because I was late, but because of internal conflict. We psychologists talk about things like internal conflict; we deal with it on a daily basis with our clients. Come to think of it, I deal with it on a daily basis with myself.

Knowing about this conflict and coaching clients on how to deal with it has been of little benefit to me. I get just as rattled and unable to handle my own stuff as before.

"Listen, what are you doing driving to see this guy?" I muttered to myself. "You have this comfortable life, a good practice, a nice big house with a nice big mortgage payment, and the world's most devoted companion. Men only mess things up. They take too much time, they take and don't give back, and pretty soon you don't know who you are any more. You twist and turn yourself to please them until you aren't you."

I considered turning back, even saw a handy street that might work as a turnaround, but traffic was heavy on Carson Street, so I kept driving.

I spied him in front of the theater, wearing his cowboy hat and looking vulnerable. He didn't see me as I sailed on past. Maybe I could plead later that I couldn't find a parking spot. Parking was dear on the South Side, especially on Saturday night.

Five minutes later, I began to panic, because there was no parking space in sight. I turned off the main street and drove several blocks on a side street before I saw the car pulling out. I waited impatiently, pulled my green cavalier into the tight spot, and then hit the road running. If I moved it, I might be ten minutes late meeting Mike.

When I reached the theater, still running and out of breath, he was smiling. "I couldn't..."

"You couldn't find a parking spot, I know. That's a legitimate excuse for tardiness here on the South Side. You should have driven over yesterday and put a chair out to hold your spot."

My breathing had quieted to small heaves of the chest. "I didn't think of that. I left home plenty early, but I forgot about the parking. Want to go in and get seats?"

He waved me ahead and I faced the woman in the ticket booth. Did he expect me to pay his way in? He didn't seem to be offering to buy my ticket. Maybe this was my penance for being late.

"One, please," I said, not feeling generous toward this man who seemed more interested in my real estate than me. Despite his saintly good humor just now, I still wasn't sure if this date would get me anywhere. My curiosity about his past lifetime counterpart had landed me here.

He bought his ticket and ushered me into the theater from behind. I glanced backward to witness his miffed expression. So he had expected me to buy his ticket—another psychological maze inside that bald head. As always, I had attracted a guy who would make an excellent client. That way I could examine heads at the office and in my off hours, too.

I shivered as if some calamity befell me in another lifetime.

"Where do you want to sit, doll?" he asked, removing his jacket, revealing a blue and white print shirt. I peered into the darkened theater that was nearly half full.

"I usually like to sit in the middle. How about you?" I crossed my fingers to ward off the incorrect response. I hate to sit in the back.

When he said, "I like to sit in the back," I must have cringed, for he continued, saying, "but maybe we can find a spot in between." He moved a few rows up from the back. "How about here?"

"Fine," I said, sorry I hadn't bought both tickets. Then I'd have a legitimate reason to insist on sitting in the middle.

My friendships with men and even women who were back forty sitters in the theater never lasted long. My intuitions about Mike were proving valid; I knew this was not only our first, but also our last movie viewing session together.

Of course there was always a home date and a movie on the DVR. That sounded even more distasteful. I couldn't imagine what boundaries he might violate. Except for our dances together in the beginning and his deep, sexy voice, if I was physically attracted to him, I was blocking it. Maybe the blonde me of that other lifetime thrilled to his touch, but I shuddered at the thought of him putting his hands on me.

"You've gotten mighty quiet, Suzanne," Mike said, putting his hand over mine.

"We're in a movie theater," I whispered. Here I was barely able to see the movie screen, parked in the wilds of the Rex Theater with some guy I didn't even like who had already begun to paw me.

"I'm going to get a drink. You want anything?" I said in desperation.

"Sure, I'll take a coke and a large buttered popcorn, heavy on the butter."

I stood by the concession stand muttering to myself. I knew Mike's type. He liked the woman to do the buying, and he would rarely offer to pay for himself, let alone for me. The only thing I hated worse than the back of the theater was a cheap guy.

With sudden inspiration, I bought two cokes and returned to where he sat. "I couldn't buy the popcorn-- couldn't carry it all with just two hands. I'll let you out if you want to get it."

"No, no, that's all right."

I settled beside him in my seat, carefully holding my coke in my right hand, the unlucky one he had held. I glanced over at him—a tiny scowl played around his mouth and eyes. I had out-operated the smooth operator.

What's wrong with you that you can't enjoy the company of an interested man and a little hand holding? Why was I so cynical? Maybe Mike was at heart a really great guy and would make a fun companion for me. Shouldn't I give him a chance?

I grew absorbed in the movie, drawn in by the characters and filming. The scenery was beautiful, a lush summer setting of country, flowers, and green fields. Just as I became engrossed in the plot and forgot about my own panorama of troubles, Mike leaned over to me.

"Could you loan me five dollars?"

"What?"

"I think I'll go get the popcorn. I'm a little short of cash right now."

I fumbled in the dark with my purse, and then handed him the bill. After he had gone, my mental attitude returned to its former state of cynicism. Not only did he get me to pay for the popcorn, but he'd probably forget to give me the change. He was very cheap, probably needy, and other than the movie, I knew I'd rather be at home with my dog. At least she had genuine feelings of love and concern for me.

Finding out about the past wasn't so easy after all. I hoped Mike stood in a long, long line at the popcorn stand. Better yet, maybe he would take the five dollars and go on home; maybe I should have given him ten so he'd go away for good.

Chapter Fourteen

ollowing the movie, which had been very touching, Mike had suggested we come to this restaurant, just a few miles from the theater. We sat at the window watching people passing by here at the Cheese Cellar, one of the shops at Station Square, down by the river.

Though I wouldn't have ordinarily continued the date, given my dark feelings about Mike the moocher, I still needed to somehow connect him with the Mike in my crystal ball and search for relevance. My gut feeling was that this connection was vitally important to discover since I had so little to go on now.

I sat back in a dark wooden chair and placed my hands on the white tablecloth. I'd shed my black down parka, revealing jeans and purple turtleneck. Street lights outside showcased swirling flakes that were accumulating, and I appreciated this warm space, reflectively quiet this evening.

He had removed his coat and cowboy hat, and his white slacks and blue Hawaiian print shirt reminded me of warmer times. In the subdued lighting, his cheekbones were accentuated, the lines of his face strengthened, so that I might have found him appealing.

We were glancing at menus, chatting about the movie, and I somehow grew comfortable in his presence. A little white candle flickered happily from the center of our table; two carnations blossomed from a bud vase beside it.

The flickering candle, the flowers, the emotions engendered by the movie, my anxiety about this Mike and the past one—they all seemed to blend and evaporate into this one magical moment. Everything was all right, just for now, and I forgot to worry, to anticipate the worst.

Somehow, everything was going to be all right.

Mike was talking about his work doing market research, which required many long hours on the telephone. His descriptions interested me, but if any more minutes slipped by, I might lose my nerve. Now was the moment to steer the conversation, to obtain valuable information, the only reason I had come here with this man. I hadn't met him so I could buy him popcorn, and without a doubt, dessert, too.

"I've enjoyed hearing about your work and find it interesting. As a psychologist, I've encountered some fascinating subjects lately. One thing that keeps coming up is the idea of reincarnation. Every way I turn, the idea keeps popping up, and I can't seem to escape it. Is that something you've ever thought about?" My heart was thumping wildly, radiating up to my throat. The hairs on my arms stood out.

"Reincarnation. Funny you should bring that up. You know I'm from a strict Catholic upbringing, grew up on the South Side, a Catholic or Orthodox Church on every street

146

corner. On Sunday morning, all those church bells rang and the gold domes shone brightly in the sun." He gazed off toward the river and sighed. I'd grown calmer now.

"And your thoughts on reincarnation?" I wouldn't tolerate digressions.

"Sorry, couldn't help but divulge my religious heritage. Anyway, just lately a man moved into an apartment in my building. He's from India, and we hit it off right away. Once in a while we get together, drink a few beers, and toss our thoughts around. Until I met Harry, I never thought too much about past lives. He's the one who got me on to that. He believes big time in reincarnation. Catholics usually aren't too strong in that area."

"I'm Protestant, myself, but I've been pointed strongly in the direction of those beliefs. Have your discussions with Harry given you any ideas?"

"Right after we first discussed it, I started paying more attention to my surroundings. It first hit me at that dance, the one I met you at."

"The swing dance at Heaven?"

"Yeah, that's the one. It was right after I saw you and danced with you. I was sitting on the sidelines watching the band play. Then I had this eerie moment when time seemed to stand still."

"What kind of eerie moment?"

"It was as if everything in the room was whirling, like a glass paperweight with snowflakes in it, then it all stopped.

147

Light pulsed from inside the room, as if there was an aura around everything I saw. And I felt connected to it all, especially to that era, the Big Band era. It was as if I had lived before in that time and I was looking back upon it, remembering somehow. Like the light was taking me back there.

"That episode gave me the shivers," he said, taking a big drag of his coffee.

Corresponding tingles shot up and down my spine. "How about since then? Have you had any experiences after that?"

"Nothing like that. Mostly I get little creeping feelings, like when I'm dancing. Feelings about being back in time, in the 1940's. Like I belong there. Actually, I those feelings happened to me before, like when I watched an old movie from then, but I didn't pay attention to them. Now, it all fits together." He smiled at me.

I smiled weakly back, wondering where this all led me. I took one more shot at the problem. "Mike, have you had any information more specific than that? Seen any flashbacks of your past, remember where you lived or who you knew?"

He shook his head slowly back and forth. "No, just these feelings. I don't know who I was, what I did, or where I lived. It's all vague, so that I'm not sure I believe any of this stuff.

"But it's also hard not to believe in this, if you know what I mean." He raised his eyebrows, and I laughed, and for that moment I felt once more at ease.

"So," he said, looking me full in the face, "Miss Suzanne, what experiences have you had with this reincarnation business? Who did you know back in time?"

I noisily spat out the hot tea I had been sipping, spraying my turtleneck and the table.

"Looks like I hit a nerve there," Mike said as I dabbed at my shirt with the napkin. He mopped at the table.

"No, not really." I smiled bravely and tried to regain composure. "You just caught me off guard. I wasn't expecting you to ask about my experiences."

"So, what are they?" His stare grew more intense by the moment.

I don't know why I hadn't anticipated this turn of plot. My lame smile covered as I worked on my shirt with little success, stalling a few minutes. I hadn't concocted a story in advance, and the truth wouldn't work. I still didn't trust Mike enough to pour out my dilemma. For all I knew, Mike was the one Teddy had left the spirit world to warn me against. On the other hand, Mike was immature and a manipulator, but he didn't seem dangerous. For an instant, I weighed the pros and cons.

I couldn't risk telling him the true story.

"I learned about past lives when I was studying psychology in California. In school we learned about all sorts of ideas and therapies I'd never heard of. I'd heard of reincarnation, but I'd never thought about it. In school, I took a course in hypnosis and past life regression, so I did some work with it then. I came up with some information about myself, but I wasn't sure if it was anything I believed."

"You said you'd been thinking about reincarnation recently, that the idea kept popping up. Your college experience probably wasn't recent. Is there something else you're not telling me?" Mike had leaned back in his chair and was chewing on a straw. So he was shrewd as well as cheapo. I wished I was better at lying.

"You're a good listener. A friend of mine took me shopping with her in Shadyside, and there were crystal balls. The shop owner said they could be used for scrying, to look into one's future or past lives."

"The old gypsy fortune teller routine? Did you buy one?"

"I thought about it." I knew I was on dangerous ground. "Then I saw an advertisement for a conference on past life regression in one of my magazines. It all seemed to fit together."

"Where's the conference?"

"It's on the island of Kauai. It's for a week, but there's time not scheduled so you can sightsee. The package looked very attractive."

"So, are you going?"

"No, I don't think so. I hate to leave my practice for a week, and then I have the puppy, too. I'd worry about her. I just found the idea interesting. You even get educational credits for going." I hoped I wasn't embellishing the story too much. I'd fabricated the conference story to divert his attention from the crystal ball. I almost wished the story was true; I needed a vacation.

"I guess something like that would be really expensive," he surmised as he studied his nails.

"Oh, surprisingly not. The whole week was $2000, and that includes air, hotel, and conference. It's very tempting." I surprised myself with the additional information. My fiction was becoming a little too ready and free flowing for someone who prided herself on being truthful.

"That kind of money amounts to a fortune to a guy like me. You psychologists must be rolling in the bucks."

I just laughed and forked the last bite of moist, rich carrot cake. "Rolling in the bucks isn't exactly accurate. I'm still paying off my educational loans."

"And here I thought you might attend the conference on Tahiti and take me along as your guest."

"Kauai. And I like to attend conferences alone so I have some quiet place to regroup and restore my energy. Besides, I barely know you. Why would I pay your way on vacation or anywhere else?" His remark annoyed me mostly because I knew he meant it. It wasn't a joke.

"I'd show you a good time," he said, clearing his throat noisily.

"What do you mean by that?" I knew, but wanted to put him on the spot.

"You know, a good time. In bed." His right leg jiggled as his brow furrowed.

151

"So you're saying you're some kind of stud. Or maybe a gigolo. You pimp yourself for free trips." I couldn't resist the opportunity to needle him.

At first he looked blank, and then he brightened up. "That's right," he said. "I'm hot in bed and the ladies show their gratitude in material ways."

"Please forgive me for saying this, but in my experience and that of my female friends, we've found that the men who advertise the loudest about their sexual prowess are generally less than adequate in bed." A sunny smile hovered about my lips.

"Look, Suzanne, I don't know how our conversation degenerated this far, but I'd like to talk about something else."

"But you were the one who wanted the free trip to Kauai compliments of me."

"Forget I said that. You dames are always taking things too seriously. A guy's just trying to have a little fun and ends up getting insulted. Of course I don't expect women to take me on trips. I always pay my own way."

I yawned and stretched. "Are you ready to go, Mike? Shall we split the bill?"

He reached for his wallet, opened it, and frowned.

"Would you mind getting it? I'm a little short of cash right now.

Chapter Fifteen

I awoke early Monday morning, my sleep especially deep and refreshing, as if I'd bathed in a remote waterfall. Princess, sensing my movements, flung her upper body on the bed and licked my arm in greeting. I was happy to be awake, to be living my life as a psychologist with this home and companion.

I sat up, leaning back against the pillows, and Princess joined me in the bed. I'd recently decided to keep her off the bed and the couch. She knew this was against the rules, but she also knew when my defenses were the weakest. I petted her vigorously, suddenly sure that this would be a lucky day for me.

Why should this day be luckier than any other? I knew my hunches were often right, so I decided to pay attention to the fine details of my life, in case I missed some opportune moment.

Next, I addressed the dog wiggling her hair onto my bed sheets. The best way to get her off the bed was to send her on a job. With eyes closed, I made a picture of Princess bringing me Mr. Baseball Bat. Our work with telepathic commands was ongoing. I held my breath as she jumped down and disappeared from the room. I heard her trotting down the stairs, then bounding back up.

Slowly, I opened my eyes. She stood just beside me with a rolled up dog sock in her mouth.

"Good girl, Princess. Very close, too. Next time you'll get it right." She stretched out and lay on the floor mouthing the black sock.

I jumped up and memories of Mike wafted through my brain, even though it was thirty-six hours later. My thoughts turned me slightly sick, and more than anything, I wanted him out of my head.

"That Mike," I said to Princess, who couldn't possibly understand my dilemma. "Mike the loser, Mike the user. I think I'm barking up the wrong tree with him.

"Besides, I can't get any information on the past out of him. He's clueless. If he does know something, he's hiding it very effectively. That's it." A weight lifted off me as I made this decision, and I knew my choice would prove right. Slightly elated, I threw on a stunning black sweat outfit for the morning romp, and then raced downstairs with my buddy.

Sometimes she let me win, but not this morning. She was waiting in the kitchen by her blue plastic food bowl. She immediately began to paw at it, knocking it about, as she barked continuously.

"I never saw another dog who got this excited over plain old dog chow." Every morning the same barking and pawing ritual, the same bowl of chow. I filled her bowl from a big bag in the cupboard and set it down before her. She attacked it vigorously, her crunching filling the kitchen.

"This stuff must be the filet mignon of dog chow," I mumbled, watching her with her pellets. When she'd finished, which was in no time at all, I threw on my coat, snapped her purple leash to her collar, and headed out the back door.

We walked through our grassy back yard to the gravel drive, and then I heard James's voice. I had half expected to hear from him.

"Wait for me, gang," he said, and jogged over to join us. Princess greeted him with some hearty tail wagging. Wearing tan slacks and his green parka, he looked alert and handsome as ever.

"Good timing. We've just started out to the park."

He greeted and caressed Princess, who sat down and offered a paw to shake. Then we were off, trotting down the narrow road that ran behind our properties.

"Except for this serendipitous moment, I haven't run into you much, Suzanne. Have you been away from home lately?"

"I haven't been on a trip or anything, but I have been out and about. I worry about Princess being alone so much, but so far she's surviving. When I'm home, I pour on the attention, that quality time thing."

"I'm right next door. Any time you need me to take the dog, I'd be glad to. I think she's a great dog," he said, and I knew he was sincere in his offer. Such a thoughtful neighbor—I couldn't help but love him.

155

"I might take you up on that, although my social life is about to take another nose dive."

"What do you mean by that?"

"I met a guy at the swing dance named Mike. He wanted to get together, so I saw him twice, and it was a disaster. I woke up today with bad vibes about him echoing in my head." I shivered just thinking about him.

"The guy with the red truck?" James asked casually.

"The one and only. I didn't think you'd met him."

"I just noticed the red truck, didn't really see the guy—wearing a cowboy hat, I think. I'd say guys in red trucks wouldn't be your thing, Suzanne."

I laughed. "I guess you're right. I only went out with him because he looked like this other guy."

"What other guy?" James sounded mildly interested.

I paused, knowing I couldn't share my story about scrying, not with anyone, not even James. "A guy I knew a long time ago. I met Mike at a dance and he looked like a twin. So I went out with him because I was curious."

"What did you find out?"

"He wasn't the man I used to know, that's for sure. I don't know what I expected to find out."

We walked into the park, which was covered with soft snow. I leaned back and admired my favorite trees—a distinguished Chinese elm here, a towering maple there. The sunlight illuminated the white covering their leaves, and I was comforted, as always. The trees had become my old friends—wise and stable, always there for me.

"What about Mike from the dance, the one you went out with? What did you learn about him?" James was holding Princess by the leash, and her head turned as she scanned the trees for squirrels.

"I learned that if I'm not excited about getting together with a man, I should listen to my intuition and not see him. Mike comes across as a user; he kept wanting me to pay for everything."

"Not a very good first impression, I would say. Sounds like a cheap guy." James's grin extended from ear to ear, as if he couldn't be happier.

"These guys just aren't wonderful like you, James. You're a true original." I patted his back and enjoyed teasing my friend.

He smiled down at me half-heartedly, and I was amazed that I'd hit a sore spot. Since I wasn't his therapist, I didn't know what to say, so I just kept walking and squelched my impulse to reassure him or delve deeper. Better not to tease him on this subject again, and yet I wasn't sure what I'd said that was offensive.

We walked and talked, meandering back along the aging sidewalk between the busy street and houses. When we came to the two Victorians, we walked up the concrete stairs to mine, James branching off to the right.

"So I hope you'll be around more, Ms. Suzanne."

"There's a high probability of that. I'm having a moratorium on questionable guys, so my social calendar is pretty blank. Do you know what I like about you?"

"What might that be?" He was poised to step onto the big wrap-around porch of his house.

"You take great delight in just walking the dog. It's refreshing."

He smiled and was gone into the house. We stepped onto our porch, opening the front door. I unhooked her leash, and Princess charged through the living and dining room, her toenails clicking, probably to attack her water dish in the kitchen.

The mail lay splayed on the rug from being shoved through the door slot. I bent down and gathered it, which included an impressive collection of advertisers and junk mail. One weather-beaten magazine had barely made it through the mail slot. I examined the torn cover and discovered a psychology magazine dated from several months ago.

It must have been adrift in the postal system, maybe stranded in some remote location, the tides eventually washing it home to me. The magazine opened to a half page color advertisement entitled "Conference in Exploring Past Lives."

I sat at the dining room table and skimmed through the information. Here was a conference aimed at psychologists, but also available to others who were interested. The conference ran for a week, and it was being held on Kauai. The seminar would start in about two weeks.

My jaw dropped, and I reread it twice till it sunk in—my fabrication to Mike had come true.

"Maybe I was connecting with the collective unconscious," I said to Princess, whose chin hairs were soaked and dripping on the floor from her water bowl visit. "I lied about this past life regression seminar on Kauai, but only under pressure, and it really existed after all. Maybe they still have openings.

"It's too much of a coincidence for this to be anything other than a spiritual journey. Better yet, I might even learn the information I need to stay alive. This could be the good luck coming my way." I looked at the price list and got excited again. It was about the same price I had quoted to Mike.

"Princess, I have to check it out," I said, feeling light and free at the idea. I hadn't been away since a Bahamas trip with a boyfriend who was fuzzy in my memory by now. He hadn't wanted to do anything other than sit in the casino, but I had explored the island, and the palm trees had been intoxicating.

An island, the garden isle of Hawaii, complete with palm trees galore. I must have been a brown-skinned native in a former life, because the island life frequently beckoned to me.

I left the magazine on the dining room table in a conspicuous spot so that I could examine it again and make a quick decision. Suddenly, getting away from my much loved home sounded appealing, as well as leaving behind crystal balls, blonde visions, Mike look-alikes, Mike himself, and a client attracted to me who raged at women.

"I signed up for a trip to Kauai, James," I told him the next day. Morning was still golden and shining through the screened walls of the gazebo behind his house. We often met here, especially in the morning or evening for hanging out. James was a chatty sort of guy.

"So you're going to Hawaii. What's the occasion?" He was standing, looking tall and handsome, leaning against a chair.

"Even though I don't need another bill, there's been a lot of stress lately, and I could use a complete change of scenery. There's a seminar on past life regression."

"What's that?" James asked, a strange look on his face, not one of his usual smirks.

"Sometimes psychologists use that tool when treating a patient. The idea is that a problem in the present may be rooted in the client's past. The past can mean his or her childhood or a past lifetime experience."

"Do you really believe that stuff?"

"I'm just thinking this might work with my patients. I'd like to expand on my present knowledge. Another tool never hurts," I said, covering my tracks, hugging my secrets to myself. "I don't know, James, what I believe in at this point. I just find this seminar interesting and because of its location, very compelling."

160

"Are you going by yourself?" James asked, examining the zipper of his gray jacket.

"Do you mean am I taking Mike?"

"Yes, sort of."

"The answer is no, a definite no, although he mentioned women paying his way on trips. I wouldn't take that man on a trip across the street."

He grinned. "You're going by yourself?"

"I'll not be alone with all the workshops and the other participants. I usually meet interesting people at these events."

"What will you do with Princess?" he asked, suddenly struck by the mechanics of the situation. "Do you want me to take her?"

"Oh, would you mind? I could take her to a kennel, but she's never been in one and she'd get much better care from you."

"Sure, I'd be glad to watch her for you. We'll have a great time." His enthusiasm warmed my heart.

"That eases my mind. I won't worry if she stays with you." This had been my main concern when scheduling the trip. I sighed and relaxed in my chair, content that I could go without a major guilt crisis.

"You go and get a rest in a beautiful tropical setting. Wallow in the sun, the beach, the ocean. Don't worry about Princess and me. We'll be just fine."

"You sound like you want to come along. Are you trying to make me feel guilty?" I kept a straight face, but was laughing on the inside.

"I'm not a psychologist, so I wouldn't fit in at your conference, but I have the heart of an island warrior."

I snorted in spite of myself.

"Oh, all right, Suzanne, you go. I'll sacrifice and stay home with the dog. If she wasn't such a nice dog, I might mind. I'll keep the aloha torches burning here in Crafton."

"Mahalo, James."

"Did you just tell me to go suck on a pineapple?"

"No, James."

Chapter Sixteen

I pulled back the two sets of maize curtains and opened the sliding glass door to reveal balmy air and a view of two tennis courts. I caught a glimpse of the ocean hiding behind another wing of the hotel. And the sky blazed full of hope--cobalt blue with bursts of sturdy white clouds, the sun reigning over all.

I sighed and sat on one of two small deck chairs on my little porch, or lanai. Beyond lay rows and rows of palm trees. My definition of the perfect vacation spot always included these swaying, exotic trees. Not only were they below my porch vantage point, but in the near distance a whole field of them— tall, graceful coconut palms planted a century ago.

I sipped at a cup of Kona decaf brewed in the comfort of my room; the coffee tasted rich and mellow, every bit as good as it smelled. The journey by airplane had seemed long, and last night I had crashed early on my double bed. But today the world was new, and Kauai awaited me, a magical island filled with passion and beauty.

The horrors receded into the distance. None of it seemed possible—the story revealed by my crystal ball of the blonde me, dead in the past, the Mike doppelganger and his possible part in the melodrama. Then there was Mike himself and his grasping ways, and the mystery of Brad and his violence with girlfriends, his professed interest in me.

Here on this island of glittering waters and trees bending casually in the wind, none of it seemed real. I'd retreated to a safe place, an oasis amidst the mysteries of my life. Somehow I knew no harm could come to me here.

I looked at my watch, carefully turned back six hours from Pittsburgh to this time zone: seven a.m. It seemed like I'd been up all morning already. The conference started at eight.

For a brief second I thought I'd do it, just stride through the hotel lobby, jump into my red Grand Am rental car and vanish down a two-lane road. The conference didn't sound interesting any more.

I had aloha fever.

A few minutes before eight, I strolled through the hotel lobby, but not out to the car. A hallway led back to the Paddle Room, where dark, wooden doors were opened wide.

Two friendly middle-aged women sat at a table decorated with white skirt inside the entryway. As I registered, I could hear generalized chatter coming from the inside room. A photograph of the workshop leader smiled at me from a bright orange poster on the registration table, depicting a sincere-looking man with bushy black hair and mustache. "Take a trip back in time; Past Life Regression" was written below his picture.

I stared at the man's name: Adrian Stein. In my scrutiny of the magazine ad back in Pittsburgh, I'd paid more attention to the hotel and its location than to the conference itself. Past life regression was certainly an interest of mine at the present moment. As I finished signing in, something caught in my throat.

Now that I'd escaped the turmoil in my life, did I really want to go to the seminar and stir up more unrest?

"Come along, pretty island lady. You want to sit by me?"

A comforting hand was at my elbow, and I turned to the man beside me who had also just finished registering. A pleasant surprise awaited me, for he radiated masculinity in his white slacks and navy and white hibiscus print aloha shirt. His easy smile, dark brown eyes alive with spirit, and casually arranged black hair took my breath away; he looked native Hawaiian. I was instantly attracted to him, and an odd feeling of familiarity inhabited the fringes of my mind.

I must have hesitated too long or have gone into shock, for a slight smile played about his lips.

"Sure," I said quickly, "I'd love to sit with you. You're the only person in this room I know." I smiled at him, making a quick recovery.

We moved into the main part of the room, staring at the ocean through windows on either side of the main platform. There were a few empty seats in most parts of the room.

"Where shall we sit?" he asked.

"How about over there?" I saw two seats at the middle table at one side. We slipped into the red padded chairs amidst the chatter of the room.

"Maybe I should introduce myself, even though we already know each other. I'm Suzanne Westin." I extended my hand. He took it and kissed it lightly while I came near to fainting.

"I'm Don Ho," he said. I strained to look at his name tag, which read "Sam Pahinui, PhD."

"I think they spelled your name wrong, Mr. Ho. It's awfully nice of you to take time out and mingle with us mainlanders. I never expected to meet a celebrity." I lowered my voice to a whisper. "I thought you had passed away."

"Yes, but I still entertain at night. After they've had a few drinks they don't remember that I'm dead. By the way, where do you practice?" he asked, suddenly getting serious.

"My show biz act?" I shot him a dazzling smile.

"I asked for that one. I'm Sam," he said, shaking my hand. "I assume we're all psychologists. Are you from the islands?"

"As far from the islands as you can get—Pittsburgh, Pennsylvania. What about you?"

"This island is my home. I was born here, just left for school and came right back. I have Kauai in my blood, can't get it out."

"So you practice psychology here?"

"Yes. I've built up a decent practice. Some of the locals can't pay much, but there are those who have moved here from the mainland either year-round or for part of the year. I manage to get by." Being analyzed by Sam Pahinui sounded enormously appealing to me, and not for therapeutic reasons.

The room had begun to quiet, and I glanced up to the front, admiring our view of the ocean. The man from the poster sat on a chair, wearing a red golf shirt and tan pants. A woman in a trim navy suit stood at the podium. She got right to business.

"Welcome all of you, and aloha, to our past life workshop. We are pleased to have a real expert in this field. He has practiced psychotherapy for twenty years, engaging in past life regressions throughout all that time.

"He has written several books on the subject, including *Where were You Two Lifetimes Ago?* and *Past Lives and Present Behavior*. Direct from San Francisco, let me introduce you to Dr. Adrian Stein."

The applause was warm, and it looked like more than a few people in the room knew Adrian from their hoots and energetic clapping—knew him and greatly admired his work. He stood up, shorter than I expected, and walked to the podium. He adjusted his trendy glasses, his face full of life, his brown hair thinning at the forehead, complemented by a brown beard and mustache. He radiated energy with a dazzling smile as he raised his hands with a look of appreciation for this audience.

167

"Thank you. It's gratifying to be here. A workshop anywhere raises my energy level and invigorates me, but a workshop here on beautiful Kauai—it's indescribable.

"Our subject has always fascinated me, ever since I was very young. I had dreams as a boy, dreams of other lives, and I always felt the information was true. Over the years I've come to believe those lives were real, and my journey has been very exciting, delving into my own personal past.

"But what has this to do with you? How can this apply to you as psychologists?

"My experience has been that our present problems and stumbling blocks can be deeply rooted in past lives. To return to the appropriate past life can most effectively solve the problem—either yours or your client's. That is the subject I hope to convey during this workshop. The methods we will use to access past life information are diverse and will be discussed later.

"But first, let me share information about the history of past life regression." As he talked, I listened intently to a man who knew his subject well and thrived on it. I found myself drawn into the story, immersed in it. But even with my absorption in this topic and the exciting speaker Adrian Stein, I was all the while aware of the man beside me.

Sam Pahinui exuded sexuality.

"Want to take a walk outside?" Sam asked gently when Adrian announced our first break.

"You read my mind," I said, eager to spend time outside in this paradise. As we followed the crowd out the center aisle, we passed Adrian Stein where he stood talking with a small cluster and men and women. To my great surprise, he placed a detaining hand on my arm.

"I don't believe we have met before. Welcome to the past life regression seminar. I'm—well, I guess you know who I am," said Adrian Stein, looking straight in my eyes. Sam hovered at my side.

My face felt sunburned, and my mind grappled with this unexpected attention as I responded, "I'm pleased to meet you, Dr. Stein. I'm Suzanne Westin. This is my best friend on the island, Sam Pahinui."

Sam nodded, a noncommittal smile about his lips.

"I'm enjoying the conference very much, Dr. Stein. Thank you for having it," I said.

"It's Adrian, dear, and I look forward to getting to know you better. These workshops are a great way to meet interesting people." he said. The intensity of his gaze confused me more than anything.

I nodded and smiled, moving on ahead to the door of the room, Sam's hand at the back of my waist. When we passed on outside, I heaved a big sigh.

"I think Dr. Adrian Stein is interested in you," Sam said. "I can't blame him."

We moved through the deserted Royal Coconut Lounge to the courtyard overlooking the pool. The sunlight warmed and energized me.

"I don't know why that upset me, the special attention from the teacher," I said.

"Maybe you knew him in a past lifetime," Sam offered soberly.

I laughed and hugged him quickly. "I need to learn about this past lifetime stuff, and I'll use it personally and professionally, but you can carry a good thing too far. I do believe our present lives are a little more important."

"I agree with you, Suzanne, although I'm here because certain events in my life pointed me toward past life regression. And the conference was handy, right on my island here." He smiled and I caught my breath—he looked so sincere and gorgeous.

"Actually, it was my personal life, too, that brought me here. And the need to escape reality and get away," I said.

"What happened to bring you here?"

I hesitated a few minutes before deciding to trust this man.
The danger was at home, not here. I didn't believe that he was in any way involved with my past life drama.

"It must have been a tense situation," he said. I knew he'd be a sympathetic listener, this island counselor.

"It doesn't even seem real any more, not here in this beautiful tropical setting. It all seems like a dream." I motioned to another brown vinyl chair, and we settled at a table beneath a brown and tan striped umbrella.

"It began, I suppose, when I bought my house. It's a beautiful Victorian built near Pittsburgh, Pennsylvania. I got a puppy and was blissfully happy, except I couldn't sleep very well. I bought this crystal ball and decided scrying might help my problem. Do you ever scry, Sam?"

"I use a mirror. Doesn't require an expensive quartz sphere. And I just began lately, too. In fact, that's why I came to this. But please continue your story." He put a reassuring hand on my arm.

"Suddenly, I'm in the middle of a murder mystery, only it's set in the past, in the Big Band era. I'm thrust onto the dance floor and hear a pretty blonde woman sing who's later greeted by a man who obviously loves her. I get a strong feeling that the woman was me, and I even see her in a house that looks amazingly like mine.

"Meanwhile, I go to a real life swing dance and encounter a man who looks like the one in the crystal ball. I go out with Mike because I want to learn about the past, but I mostly learn Mike likes to use women." I smoothed my tan shorts and deep pink top with one hand as I spoke.

"In another scene from my scrying, I see the blonde lying dead in the woods. Have I made any sense with this? It sounds like a bunch of gibberish to me."

"It's interesting, and I understand the gist of what you're saying. Who would have wanted to kill the woman?" His

171

concentration was gratifying, and I wondered if this man ever took a day off.

"There was another scene where she's with another man in the house, an unattractive man, actually. They're kissing, and then go up the stairs. I'm not sure what this other man is about. He gives me the creeps and I don't know what she sees in him."

"Have you been doing a lot of scrying since this all began?"

"Every chance I get, but the information comes in spurts. It's the story of love, betrayal, and violence. I'm very near discovering the whole truth." Or at least I hoped so.

"Why is this story significant for you now? Why does it upset you?"

I told him about Teddy and his prophecy of danger.

He sat thoughtfully, absorbing all this information. "I can see why you wanted to escape. Kauai can help you forget. At the same time, it sounds like you need to solve your puzzle. Sometimes pushing straight ahead into the thick of trouble can be the best answer."

"What about you, Sam? What's your story?"

With a scraping sound, he pushed his chair back from the table, stood up, and stretched. "I will be glad to tell you, but we're well past the break time. Dr. Stein will be coming out here to look for you. We'd better go in."

"Maybe we should cut class," I said, eyeing the brilliant day and the ocean waters tumbling onto the sand. Even from here, I could hear the murmur of the restless waves and smell the sea salt.

"Oh, Suzanne, how you tempt me," he said, taking my hand. "Come along, my beautiful temptress. Let us assimilate the knowledge we came here to learn. Let us go back into the Paddle Room and watch Dr. Adrian Stein strut upon the stage."

"You're right," I said. "I surrender to the forces that have brought me here to this island. So let's paddle off to the Paddle Room."

"Mahalo, wahine," he said, looking very Hawaiian.

"Does that mean I have dirt on my shorts?" I asked, checking them as I stood to go.

Chapter Seventeen

I awoke early the next morning, but late by my internal Pittsburgh clock. It was just getting light outside, as I saw through the filmy curtain covering the sliding glass door to my lanai. The digital clock by the bed announced current island time: 6:37.

Without a trace of lethargy, I flung the bed covers aside and stood to stretch. The room's comforts pleased me, including the perfect temperature and blessed quiet. Best of all, I eagerly anticipated this second day in a tropical wonderland, despite the confines of the conference.

The workshop offered a buffet breakfast when it reconvened at 8 a.m., but my stomach cried out now. I threw on shorts and tank top, grabbed a coconut muffin I'd bought at the Safeway and hustled out the door with my camera.

In my casually disheveled state, I hoped I wouldn't run into anyone I knew. Come to think of it, I hardly knew anyone here, so was sure to be safe. Something drew me out here, and I didn't want to miss whatever it was. In a few minutes I'd walked through the courtyard to the beach. When I looked up at the sky, my hunch to hurry out was perfectly validated.

The clouds and sun had combined to speak strongly to my soul. Potent shades of blue and gray lit the clouds, as sun beams shot strongly through, an early morning display of mystical power and truth.

I took three shots with my little point and shoot camera, hoping the beauty of this sunrise would translate. Then I sat down on a bench facing the ocean to absorb this scene. And munched on my coconut muffin, which was moist and heavenly.

The light skittered off the waters as this sunrise overshadowed all others I'd watched in my life (granted, not that many). The energy was so magnetic that I searched the distant sky, almost expecting angels to descend from the clouds. The light and clouds metamorphosed as I sat there, entranced. I must have concentrated fiercely, for when the hand touched my shoulder, I jumped.

"Didn't mean to scare you. Mind if I join you?" he said from behind me. I recognized the voice as I gulped down the rest of my muffin in paradise.

"No, please sit down, Dr. Stein. I've been watching the sky. It's so beautiful."

"And so are you, Suzanne. Please call me Adrian. I don't like to get too heavy on the authority figure thing." Adrian was the only other person in sight. Evidently, not many guests were up and about at this hour.

"Are you glad you came to Kauai, Suzanne? Are you having fun?"

175

"Oh, yes, this is a real change from my routine at home. The conference is very interesting. I'm learning a lot. I'm just wishing I could do more sightseeing of the island. If I disappear for a while, you mustn't think badly of me." I wasn't sure how he would take this, but it was exactly how I felt. I was anxious to see the sights and get close to this island and its people.

"Let me see," Adrian said, and I studied him up close. A small man, he appeared to be in his forties, with only a few gray hairs sprouting amidst his hair, including the beard and mustache. His build was compact, yet sturdy, and looked like he worked out, and his face, arms, and legs sported a healthy tan, as if he spent time outdoors.

His eyes shone a startling green, as full of life and charisma as the spectacle of the clouds and sun just now. I couldn't help being drawn to him in spite of myself.

"I know," he said. "We could tour the island this afternoon when the lunch break starts."

"What about the conference? We're scheduled until three o'clock today. How can the show go on without you? You're the star." The idea amused and surprised me.

"I have some movies they can show. They're movies about past life regressions and are actually quite good. I've used them before to get a little break."

"Now Dr. Stein, I paid my money to learn at this conference. In fact, it's of utmost importance to me. My life may depend on it." I hadn't expected to lay bare my soul with Adrian.

"What does that mean, young lady? You look as if you don't have a care in the world."

"You can't count on looks. I'm a psychologist, busy with my private practice. After I bought a house, I began scrying with a crystal ball and discovered me in a past life dead in the woods. And along with that, I received a warning that I was in danger now. That's the short version."

"This is more intriguing than the average story. Your scrying has alerted you to personal danger. But who would want to harm you?" He slid an arm around my shoulders, not exactly a fatherly gesture.

"You talk as if you know me, and I can't help but question the personal attention you've been giving me. I'm just another workshop attendee trying to learn something that will apply to my practice and possibly save my life. What's going on?" I slid over away from him on the bench.

He looked a little sheepish. "You know it's getting a little hot out here in the sun." He pulled at the neck of his T-shirt. "Let's move to the shade."

We moved back toward the pool beneath a table with the beige and brown beach umbrella. I smiled over at him and he shifted uncomfortably in his seat.

"No one ever called me on my extracurricular interests before. I've had women give me stern faces before they

177

retreated, but mostly I get admiration and respect when I meet ladies at the conferences. I enjoy the closeness.

"I usually spot one special person at each workshop and spend time with her, get to know her better. It makes my job more interesting, Suzanne. The ladies are usually thrilled to be chosen by me."

"And what does your wife think about all this?"

"What do you mean?" He looked downward and studied the fingernails of one hand.

"I think you have a wife and children," I said, following probability as well as a hunch.

"Have you been studying your crystal ball? You're not some kind of witch, are you?"

"I noticed in all your bios the personal information was scanty. And now this pursuing of women at conferences. I'd say in your home life you're the kind of guy who always has a woman at his side—and probably marries her right away, too, to cement the thing."

He bowed and smiled at me. "You're a psychologist or psychic? Your portrait of me is accurate. My wife, my third wife, doesn't know about the workshop ladies. Nor did the others.

"But now, since I'm squirming here talking about an uncomfortable subject, please answer my question from before: Why would anyone want to harm you? Although with your powers of deduction, I could see how someone might want to hush you up."

"You understand that you're not a client coming to me for help or I'd talk to you differently. Plus, I expect that your position as an authority figure lends itself to extra discretion. Your fans may look up to you and not see the real person beneath the titles and credits."

"Ouch," he said. "You're avoiding my question."

"I ask myself about this one frequently. It just doesn't add up. In the past, there is a motive. The girl who was me had a husband or lover. Later, she is sexually involved with another man. Jealousy or a passionate rage would be the motive."

"But none of this applies now?"

"No, I just don't get it. I met a guy who is an identical twin to her boyfriend, but he's just someone who likes to sponge off women. I have no interest in him."

"You have some issues with men, Suzanne. You should let me help you with that." A spark of energy shot through his smile.

"You're right, and no thanks. The only other lead I have at this point is a client named Brad. He came to me because of his relationships with women. I've learned he can flip into rages and nearly strangled his last girlfriend."

"And this relates to you?"

"He asked me out. I told him no for professional reasons, but he must harbor some feelings for me."

"I see. This is all intriguing. Would you like me to hypnotize you to get more information? It *is* my specialty."

179

The barriers were crumbling as my need outweighed my assessment of his motives. "I might like that. I wouldn't want to ask for any special favors, though."

"Please. The group regressions I'll do during the workshop will be helpful, but not like a one-on-one session. I'm here to help you, and since you scorn me as a romantic lead, I can at least help you as a therapist." He stood up and put his hands on my shoulders.

"I have to prepare for this morning's session. Perhaps this evening or tomorrow evening I could regress you."

"Thank you. Yes, we can decide about that later. It's very kind of you to make that offer." I was convinced that if I didn't take advantage of his offer tonight, he'd have a new conference lady friend and little time for me.

As he left, I turned and studied the sunrise that had brought me out here. The sky was pretty, but all the magic had somehow evaporated while Adrian and I conversed. Despite that, my heart's burden had lightened after his offer of help.

Wouldn't mind more sunrises over Kauai. I suddenly realized how much I loved this place already.

Sam sat at the table we'd used yesterday looking very sexy and very Hawaiian in his black and tan print aloha shirt and tan slacks. He stared out at the ocean through the long windows of the Paddle Room, the room nearly full and noisy with early morning chatter.

"Aloha, Sam," I said, touching his shoulder.

"Aloha to you, Miss Mainlander." His smile held the energy of the sun. "Ready for another big day of delving into your past lives?"

I plunked down beside him, on his near side so that he provided a protective buffer between me and Adrian Stein.

"I'm ready to see this island, just itching to go and explore. What a dumb idea to come for a conference. I should have just come."

"Ah, but you said you need this information and need it soon. You can always come to visit again. Better yet, you could come here and live."

"I think the relaxation would do me good." My eyes scanned the crowd. It looked like everyone had come back for more and were settling down.

"Maybe we could do some sightseeing this afternoon. I could show you a few things on the island. I don't think it would hurt to miss one session of the conference."

"I'd like that, Sam. I'd be grateful to see anything. It just kills me to be here in this gorgeous place sitting away in a conference room." My heart yearned for the sun and ocean beyond the windows, and my common sense agreed.

"I'll show you around, then. Has Dr. Stein accosted you since I last saw you yesterday?"

"Actually, he approached me on the beach this morning. I told him I wasn't interested in a married guy—he is married—

and especially not a vacation fling. He still offered to do a regression on me. I might take him up on that."

"You would let him hypnotize you? Is that advisable?" Sam turned with raised eyebrows and stared into my eyes.

"It sounds all right, even though he isn't the most trustworthy guy. Sleazy might be a better term for him as he misuses his position for sexual purposes. But I do believe he's skilled in past life regressions."

"I could come and watch the guy, make sure he doesn't pull any quick tricks." Sam's face muscles tightened and belied the lightness of his tone.

"I'll be all right. You're sounding like my big brother."

"You can't be too careful, not even here in paradise," he said as Adrian Stein entered the room from the rear and walked up the aisle, right toward us. The chattering died down.

"Hello again," Adrian said to me, winking, as he broke stride, then moved on past.

Beside me, Sam released a big sigh, but I could sense his bristles rising. I patted his hand, and he sent me a lopsided smile.

Adrian greeted the audience and spoke of his experience with clients and past life regression, telling of fascinating case histories. His extensive work in the field and hundreds of regressions qualified him as a noted authority, without question. Though the man Adrian irritated me, his speech as a clinician drew me in. Mesmerized by his words, I lost track of time and place.

I forgot about being on Kauai, that the ocean and sunshine lay just beyond the wall. Enthralled with the subject matter, I existed on a fascinating plane where past lives and present ones interconnected. I could picture these men and women who journeyed back in time to seek out the answers to their problems and present miseries.

One was a man who couldn't be touched around his neck. After a few weeks of regressions, he learned of his hanging in London in the 1800's.

Early in Adrian's practice, before he had dealt with past life phenomena, he encountered a woman who had severe problems with her relationships with men. The men she gravitated toward were entirely unsuitable and unable to sustain an emotional link with her, frequently leaving her.

Adrian hypnotized her, hoping to uncover some trauma in her childhood. She began to speak of her fear of her lover. She feared for her life, and she wanted to go away from him to save herself. She didn't have the money or means to escape.

As Adrian questioned her, he learned to his surprise that she came from Germany in the early 1900's. The information she gave him in that session and others was from a past life in which her lover murdered her.

Adrian was intrigued and learned all he could on the subject.

I shuddered when hearing about the German woman. It was a little too close for comfort—a woman who couldn't sustain relationships with men, and she was murdered in a past life. It seemed unreal, and I secretly wished it was happening to anyone other than me, but I also knew that to deny reality could be fatal.

Reality always wins.

During our break, I hung out with Sam, walking outside and talking about the information. Before I knew it, the lunch break had come, and the tables above and behind us were laid out with an appetizing luncheon buffet. Fruits, especially pineapple, and salads dominated the menu.

"Let's have a little lunch, then we'll start our tour of Kauai," Sam said.

"Good plan," I said, following him, thankful we were near the head of the line. Sightseeing now ranked first in my mind.

Adrian stepped down from the stage flanked by two of the conference organizers. Stopping beside me, he cleared his throat and spoke. "Do you want to come to the front of the line with me, Suzanne? We could sit together."

"Sam and I are having lunch together, Adrian. Would you like to join us?" I sensed Sam stiffening beside me.

Adrian shook his head as he said, "Catch you later, then. See you this afternoon."

I winced. "Sam's taking me sightseeing, the non-tourist, native view of Kauai."

"What about the regression?" I could see his two escorts were starting to fidget as he conversed with me.

"If you don't mind, tonight would be great. I could meet you out by the pool at eight o'clock."

He grinned quickly and waved his two escorts ahead. "That will be fine. Meet you at eight o'clock, then. Take good care of her, mister," Adrian said, nodding toward Sam.

"The same to you, Dr. Stein. I'll be the island tour guide and you can be the guide to the journey within. Aloha."

Adrian plowed ahead to the front of the line, and Sam and I both snorted into our hands to keep from laughing out loud.

How comforting to have a brother watching over me on this island thousands of miles from home.

Chapter Eighteen

S am sent me ahead to the boat docks as he chatted with a cousin or nephew or long lost uncle at the ticket booth. The glistening Wailua River, wide as a four-lane highway, mesmerized me, as well as the motion of the boats tethered to the dock. Since I wasn't certain of my destination, I consulted a smiling, thin man who looked to be Chinese and in his fifties.

"Excuse me, but do I get on this boat?" I asked, pointing to the red boat behind him. "I'm going on the trip to Fern Grotto."

"It depends on your ticket. Which one do you have?" asked the man, grasping my ticket. "Oh, sorry, the other boat line."

I noticed now that there were a dozen flat boats painted red tethered at the dock and further down boats painted green. The green boats said "Smith Boat Line," the red, "Wailua River Boats."

"But I want to go on your boat," I said, giving him a little wave. He blew me a kiss.

Sam joined me from behind as I reached the Emy Jo, the first of the green boats. Windows lined the sides of the flat-roofed boat. A big native man in a blue and white shirt stood helping people into the boat.

"Hello, Sam," the big guy said, glancing over at me.

"Fred, how's it going?" They shook hands.

"You seem to know that guy," I said as we slid onto the bench seats that lined each side, about twenty tourists on the boat.

"I'm related to most of the natives on this island. Fred's some kind of cousin."

Fred came onto the boat and commandeered the steering wheel, turning on the engine as a man threw a rope aboard. To my amazement, as we navigated into the Wailua River, Sam grabbed a ratty-looking guitar near him and got up. He stood before a microphone and spoke to the crowd.

"We welcome you today for a cruise on beautiful Wailua River to Fern Grotto. We hope you will enjoy your time together. For your pleasure, our fine crew will entertain you on the voyage up the river.

"Please allow me to introduce Lani, our lovely hula maiden. To my left is Laloa, playing ukulele. Guiding this craft today is Captain Fred, who will fascinate you with his commentary on the trip back." The big man inclined his head and smiled at us tourists.

Lastly, Sam smiled benevolently at the people and said, "And I'm Don Ho's oldest boy, Don Ho, Jr." Applause, big smiles, and cheers broke out from the benches.

I watched and listened as Sam broke into song, making the old guitar sound better than the fancy ones at home. As Lani began her hula, I studied her closely. She looked exactly like the Lani who had danced at my hotel the night before. When her eyes touched me, her smile grew a little bigger and warmer.

Already I knew people here on this island.

Lani was lovely, a slender woman no older than thirty. With her long dark brown hair, fine features, and long blue and white flowered gown, she easily owned her part as Polynesian beauty. Her dancing was equally graceful, slender legs moving in time to the music, lithe, shapely arms, and hands that communicated in a flowing, effortless manner.

My attention drifted to the river that flowed so serenely to the ocean, deep blue or green depending on the light. This gorgeous, sunny day bewitched the water, making it alive with light, highlighting even the low-growing, emerald-colored trees that lined both banks. I inhaled deeply of the clean river water smell. The river flowed wider than I had expected; we easily passed another river boat and some kayakers, with plenty of room to spare. Everyone on this river waved to us like happy children on a school tour.

Sam and his crew performed one number right after the other, some with Lani, some without. We had ridden fifteen minutes or so before Sam requested that we all stand up. Because of his wit that gave us warm, fuzzy feelings toward him, we all stood up and awaited further instructions.

"And now, our lovely hula maiden Lani will lead you in a traditional dance, the hula. Everyone, to the count of three, step right, left foot together, then right. Then to the left with a three count. Continue moving the feet, then we add the hands. Since you all have arms and legs, this should be a cinch.

"I'll play the music, you follow Lani's hands. This hula lesson is so you can go home and teach all your friends."

Sam strummed on the guitar and broke into song. The lines of tourist-dancers swayed in time to his beat. I tried to move fluidly, and to keep the feet moving and make the appropriate gestures with my hands, but I struggled. It wasn't as effortless as Lani made it look.

When we finished, we sat down, laughter filling the flat-topped cabin. We were pulling near a landing on the bank of the river where a few kayaks were tethered.

"And now as we leave the boat to walk a short distance to the Fern Grotto, we will go as a group. After you have viewed this natural spectacular site, you will return to this boat. Don't forget the name of the boat—the Emy Jo. Captain Fred will narrate the ride on the trip back.

"So you may all disembark and we will take you to see the grotto, a favorite spot for weddings."

Captain Fred handed us out of his vessel, and I found myself just behind Lani. I chatted with her and discovered that we both recognized each other from her hula dancing at the Coconut Beach Hotel the evening before. She danced at the Coconut Marketplace as well as the hotel and boats. Already a fan, I told her how much I enjoyed her hula.

Sam appeared from behind me, looked at me, and smiled.

"That was quite a surprise, Mr. Ho. I never expected your act, which was quite entertaining, by the way. You've got a mean strum there."

"I do some fill in work, work some weekends. Everybody in Hawaii, speaking for the natives, has two or three jobs. Today I begged the regular singer to let me take his place so I could impress you. I'm working for free."

"I appreciate your efforts, Sam. Show biz suits you well. It makes me wonder how you ever got into psychotherapy."

"Strumming the guitar doesn't pay many bills, my dear wahine."

I laughed and patted his shoulder as our group, which had been waiting for a previous group to leave the grotto, started to herd ahead.

Standing beside the path with his coworkers in his red flowered shirt was the man from the other boat line who had directed me back at the docks. We recognized each other instantly. His face lit up and we said together, "It's you!" He embraced me warmly, I returning it. Such fun.

I continued with my group, again feeling a belonging to this island, feeling at home with the natives I'd met. Behind me, Sam commented, "I guess I must belong to the wrong boat line."

"What do you mean?" I asked, though I knew.

"The other guy got all the loving," he said.

"You'll get yours later. You're on duty right now—can't drink, smoke, or squeeze the ladies."

"That's the only reason I work this job—the perks." He tilted his head, a question on his face.

We had arrived at the grotto and Sam took charge, explaining the area. Made of gray rocks with a recessed area underneath, it resembled a large open cave. Ferns hung down and grew from the rocks, light green and delicate-looking, bordering on straggly. I'd read in my guidebook that hurricane Iniki had severely damaged the ferns here in 1992.

As we tourists stood in the cave under the ferns, Sam and his ukulele playing friend stayed below and sang and played a wedding song. The Hawaiian music, with its gentle cadences, was working its way into my bloodstream. The melodies were simple, but beautiful, and I knew I'd miss them, among other things, when I returned home to Pittsburgh.

As our group departed the grotto, Sam shook hands with everyone. He grasped my hand an extra half minute and spoke into my ear.

"Normally I stay and do the show on a return boat, but for you I'm changing that. I'll be returning with you on the Emy Jo," Sam said with a wink.

"There might be another reason, too," I said.

"What?"

"After all, you're not getting paid."

* * *

When we'd returned to the boat dock and all the tourists had wandered off, I turned on Sam and rewarded him and me with an enthusiastic embrace. Electricity shot though me, and passion welled up, filling me like a sweet perfume, and sexual yearning shot up like a geyser. Wild, primitive urges compelled me to step back when my body urged me forward instead. My friendly gesture, transformed to a sexual hot bed of coals, confused me.

"That was nice." His eyes were dazed, and he sighed contentedly.

"Not sure what happened there," I said lamely, heart pounding.

"Land of volcanoes, dear," he said, his eyes holding me tenderly.

"Volcanoes?" God, this man was gorgeous.

"Never know where the steam will vent, where the power will be released," he muttered as he caressed my hand.

"It's not active—dormant."

He understood my rambling. "Yes, our volcano's long since dormant, but the power remains. Can you feel it?"

"Oh, yes, I feel it. And I was going to kid you about your wife and kids," I said, attempting a recovery of my senses.

"My kids are fine. Do I seem like a family sort of guy?" He'd recovered his composure, and we began retracing our steps back toward his car.

"I don't know too many family men. As far as the wife, I think you're going through a divorce.

"How did you come up with that?" His eyes widened, and I read respect and surprise in them.

"That." I pointed to the light mark left from a band on his left ring finger.

"I see. I can't decide if you're more talented as a psychotherapist or as a detective. You're right. We have two little girls. We divorced a few months ago. I left the ring on till pretty late. I'm having a period of turmoil right now. Would you like to become involved in my turmoil?" He reached for me again, and I hopped back, waggling one finger at him.

"Turmoil is what I'm here to escape. So it wouldn't do to substitute more turmoil. Besides, I'd fall in love with you, Sam, and next thing I'd be back in Pittsburgh sobbing my eyes out. I'd never be able to eat pineapple again without crying on it."

"Poor little Suzanne." He was holding me now, ever so lightly, breathing into my hair. I'd gone tingly all over.

He released me, grabbing my hand instead.

"Since we skipped class, we'd better make the most of this afternoon, mainland lady. What do you want to see?"

"Whatever you think. I just want to see the scenery, mingle with the landscape, be a part of Kauai." I kept thinking about how good he smelled, and not from cologne.

"Hold onto your hat, lady. You get the tour reserved only for visiting dignitaries."

193

* * *

"We've come full circle," I said to Sam, who sat across from me. Our table touched the outer wall of this restaurant, and I could still see bright sunshine on the Wailua River flowing placidly by outside. Palm trees conformed to the breezes, and the scenery and this day still gave me an idyllic, heady sensation.

"Full circle? Oh, you mean we started at the morning boat ride at the marina and now we're back at the Marina Restaurant. With lots of other stops in between. I must say, Ms. Suzanne, this has been a most therapeutic day for me. I can feel the turmoil beginning to subside." He made a funny face, yet still managed to look handsome.

I smiled and watched the tour boats at the dock move gently as boat wake hit them. I could see the Emy Jo from here.

The waitress, a polite native lady, took our order, and then we surrendered our menus.

"This was a wonderful, highly therapeutic day for me, too. It chased all the demons away. I'm safe here, in this place with you. I needed to get relief from the pressures at home, even if for just a few days. Thank you so much for today, Sam."

"Which of the sights did you like best, beautiful wahine?"

"It must be the beaches, those beaches on the north shore. They were incredibly beautiful. But then, I found the Kilauea Lighthouse haunting, too. I was just glad you didn't make me hike the Kalalau Trail very far."

"It's very beautiful, but also very treacherous."

"They have a lot of nerve calling it a trail. It's more like a heap of boulders on the side of a cliff high above the ocean."

He laughed as our salads came, and we engaged in some serious crunching. I hadn't realized how hungry I was. The fresh air and our walking had whetted my appetite.

"Sam, you never told me your story." I'd nearly forgotten in all our activity.

"You mean about the divorce?"

"No, though I'd be glad to do counseling for you. Remember I told you about how I got into scrying, my experiences with it as far as past life phenomena? You promised to talk about your experiences. You said later."

"This is later?"

"Yes. We may not have time together later in the week," I said wistfully. He mattered to me already—maybe too much.

"Oh, I hope this isn't it. I need all the therapeutic days I can get. I enjoy your company, and you are a beautiful lady."

"You're stalling, but you're allowed to. I'm not complaining."

He flashed a big smile and began. "Even as a little boy, when I was awake, I would see flashes of other places and other times. My mother and father told me I had an overactive imagination, and for a while I convinced myself it wasn't real.

"Then my Grandmamma Lilli, my mother's mother, heard about it. She took me aside and talked to me. She said, 'Sam, you have a special gift and you mustn't let the others talk you

195

out of it. I think you are seeing pictures from other times. You could be seeing the past or you could be seeing the future, but the messages you are getting are about you. It is important that you pay attention to these scenes in your mind.'

"So I began to take the information seriously. Many times, especially as I got older, I would write down what I saw and my feelings about the information, my impressions. I became curious about the human mind and behavior, which led me into the study and practice of psychotherapy.

"Just recently, though, my gift hasn't been enough. When Eileen and I began to drift apart, I tried to bring us back together, with little success. Sorry I'm talking about the divorce, but the stories intersect at this point."

I nodded, engrossed in his story and said, "Please go on, Sam. This is very interesting."

"I couldn't understand what was happening to us. My gift told me nothing. I have no control over what I see or when I see it. I drew a blank.

"I've studied hypnotherapy and occasionally use it with clients, but self-hypnosis didn't appeal to me. You see, I'm certain we've all had past lives. I don't even question that. And I felt our problem, Eileen's and mine, was buried in some past conflict, unresolved for centuries, perhaps.

"I was staying in a little apartment and not enjoying myself, when one night I decided to scry. I'd bought a black plastic hand mirror at a dollar store, and in the depths of my despair, I used it with great concentration. I gazed into it for at least an hour and absolutely nothing happened.

"I got up and paced in the dining room of the apartment, and cursed my condition. I thought about throwing the mirror in the ocean. Sometimes any action seems like progress. I drove to the nearest beach, about a mile away, and prepared to hurl the mirror into the crashing surf.

"That was when I first saw it."

"What was it, Sam?" I asked softly.

"I just caught it out of the corner of my eye, a flash in the mirror as I reached back to toss it. It startled me. I brought it forward and looked and saw a soft glowing in it.

"I looked all around to see what was reflecting in my mirror, but there was nothing to explain it. I carried it back onto the beach and gazed into the mirror as pictures began to unfold, so vivid that I felt a part of the scene. It felt natural. And real," he said, catching his breath.

"Did you find the story you were seeking?" I asked, intrigued by his narrative.

"I think so. It was one of many. I don't know how long I was out there. I'm not even sure if I slept, but I was there until the sunrise, when I drug myself back to my meager apartment, a happier soul."

"Are you stalling again?" I asked, eager to hear the good part.

"Maybe. Even though I learned a story that explained my situation, that didn't change the outcome. Eileen and I divorced anyway. But for some reason I had found peace and acceptance of the situation."

I smiled and crossed my arms. The waitress appeared from somewhere behind the salad bar with our dinners. She presented me with a seafood platter that boasted everything but Moby Dick fried or broiled in an appetizing arrangement.

Sam had opted for a spaghetti dinner that somehow didn't do justice to our tropical surroundings. But after all, he did live here. Paradise must include spaghetti, evidently.

"Shall we eat? I'm still very hungry from my tour guide duties," Sam said, diving into his pasta.

"This doesn't let you off the hook. You have my curiosity wide awake and anxious for your story."

"Not to worry, beautiful lady. Right after I wolf down this pasta, you shall have your story. Boy Scout's honor." He held up three fingers in a salute.

"Were you ever a Boy Scout?" I asked.

"No," he said, and then kept on eating.

Chapter Nineteen

*M*y seafood smelled and tasted delicious, and Sam munched his spaghetti with enthusiasm. When the final bites had been consumed, we rose by unspoken mutual consent and stretched our cramped limbs. My heart had warmed toward Sam, having thoroughly enjoyed every minute of our day together.

"Are you still doing the regression with Adrian Stein?" Sam asked.

"As far as I know. That was the last plan I heard."

"When?"

"Eight o'clock. What time is it now?" Oblivious to time's passing, I glanced down at my watch.

"It's just seven o'clock now, so we don't have to rush. It'll take about ten minutes to drive back to the hotel. Shall we go back now and sit and talk there?" Sam said.

Traffic was light, and we reached the Coconut Beach Hotel in record time, but had to park in the far outback of the lot since the nightly luau was in progress. The ever popular luau and Polynesian show whittled down the free spots in the lot. We walked toward the hotel, side by side, comfortable as old friends.

"Want to walk on the beach?" I asked him. He nodded, and as we reached the sand, he began speaking of his scrying visions.

"It was ancient times, and it was here, on this island of Kauai. I recognized the geography. But none of this was here." He motioned toward the hotels and the business strip. "There were simple huts and fishing boats, nothing more. My husband and I lived together—yes, I was a woman in that lifetime—and my wife Eileen was my husband.

"We were very happy and lived a simple life with simple pleasures. We didn't aspire to be anything other than what we were. Mind you, these were pictures, but I understood them. It was almost as if I remembered those times in some part of my being.

"Though many men in our village took several wives, my husband Kaime had not. We had an understanding between us that others did not share; neither he nor I would have sex with another. Even during the festival Makahiki, when others slept with the wives and husbands of others, we did not.

"We were in our early thirties when the trouble began. In one scene I cried violently—huge, wracking sobs—and Kaime tried to comfort me. He could not console me, and my face was heavy and puffy from crying. He was bewildered and unable to understand my misery. Finally, after much beseeching, he convinced me to talk of my problem.

"He listened intently as I told of my desolation because we had no children. He had known my wishes in the past,

200

which he shared, but we mostly chose to endure this unhappiness in silence and apart from one another. I knew my days of potential childbearing were numbered.

"Besides that, two wives in our village had just announced their pregnancies. I had rushed to our hut and wept, my tears a storm that didn't wash away my anguish. The crying only made it worse.

"My husband was taken back by my display of such fierce emotion. 'But what can we do, Iolana?' he said to me. 'You have been to the medicine man who used powerful medicine on us. Nothing happened. We have beseeched the gods and left offerings and still no babies. If there's anything else we could do, I will help you. Do you wish me to take another wife to get you a baby? Please tell me what you wish me to do. You know you are my life. I care about little else.'

"As he caressed my long, dark hair, I sobbed even harder, for in my heart I had formed a plan I couldn't tell even my beloved husband. I told him I must go to a sacred place to pray that very night, and he said, 'Let me go with you. I will pray, too.'

"'I must go alone, but I will return before morning to lie with you. You must not worry or try to follow me. I will be safe. I must do this, for I am heartbroken.'

"'Very well, I will trust your judgment. I am trying to understand your longing for a child. But if this doesn't work, we can continue to enjoy each other and our life together. We may have to accept our childless condition and grow closer together. For I will be with you and take care of you and watch over you, my love.'

"As he kissed me tenderly and comforted me, I felt worse than ever, but I'd stopped crying. My loving Kaime trusted me completely, yet he didn't realize how ruthless I had become in my search for a child. How could I tell him I was willing to betray him and the trust between us to get what I wanted?

"As I packed a small bag for my trip, he lingered, then bid me good night. I left quickly, head bowed low, and fled to an isolated stretch of beach. When I got there, I could see, for the moon was full with not a cloud anywhere. The night was warm, but comfortable. I spread out a cover from my bag and waited. I sensed it wouldn't be long now.

"My prayers were of the physical sort, for after Kale arrived, we got right to business. It had been his idea after all, Kale who had fathered many children with his wives, Kale who had whispered in my ear about getting me with child.

"He didn't want me as his wife, for he had several already. It may have been carnal urging or curiosity or perhaps genuine concern at my distress. He lustily set to work at making me pregnant. A part of me went into shock and stayed there during our night together. There was physical excitement and fulfillment, I must admit, but the emotional horror kept me from anything like enjoyment of our time together.

"Yet I kissed him goodbye as dawn streaked the horizon.

"'I will be with you again, lovely lady, if you need me,' he said.

"'We will see, Kale. I will let you know.' Weary and sick of myself, I idly wondered about climbing to a cliff and throwing myself off the precipice.

"I returned home and continued my life, and when the morning sickness started and my breast become sore, I felt little joy in it. After all my longing, my yearning, and crying, I was pregnant, yet not happy about it.

"As the pregnancy advanced, I pretended to be happy. My husband, of course, was ecstatic. The baby grew inside me and got life and moved and turned, yet still my heart had become like wood.

"He was born during a terrific storm, born a strong, lusty boy, and I couldn't help but think of Kale and our lusty night together. Kale even came with his wives to see the baby, and he squeezed my hand, looking knowingly into my eyes. I turned my head as a wave of nausea rushed over me.

"What if my husband finds out, what will become of this child, I asked myself? I knew no peace. And though I tried to love the child, a part of me held back, a part of me had died at his conception.

"When my son had grown to be two he looked very much like Kale, but people said he was the image of Kaime, who was so proud of our son. But the lovely world we had built together had crumbled. I cringed now when my husband touched me, and our times together were no longer happy and free. In some

203

ways getting what I wanted had made me an even unhappier person.

"I brooded and obsessed about my indiscretion, and at last I decided to end it all. I no longer wanted to live. I walked many miles to the cliffs of the ancient trail and hurled myself off into the sea. Flying through the air, free as the birds, I was laughing right before I hit the water."

Stunned by his story, I waited briefly as he composed himself. Wild and eerie, it was, yet believable—the human condition, our emotions, and foibles. Sam had been talking for some time now, yet I needed to know more.

"What became of your son?" I asked.

"The story ends when I hit the water. I've tried to go beyond that by scrying, but without success. That's one of the reasons I've come to this conference."

"And the other reasons?"

"I must have known you were coming, Suzanne."

"Maybe so, my friend." I was touched by his comment, which had a ring of sincerity to it. "Anything else?"

"I plan to use this in my practice. I know how powerful this story was for me. I instantly understood the present conflict between my wife and me. At the same time, I knew it wouldn't be resolved, but I've started inner work to stop this from happening in a future lifetime. I even explained to Eileen about what happened, but she wasn't open to the information. Perhaps hearing it will resolve future problems. This past work is very powerful."

"I know," I mumbled, suddenly reminded of my own drama, the one I'd successfully pushed out of my mind. I shivered and Sam slipped his arm around me.

"I'm not cold. This stuff can get pretty creepy. Nervous reaction."

"I thought so." He squeezed me in a hug that shot clear to my feet. "There's something I ought to tell you, but I really don't want to."

"What is it, Sam?"

"It's almost eight o'clock and I see that snake Adrian Stein coming out through the courtyard. Can't we just duck away into the lounge somewhere?" Sam's smile had disappeared, like the sun beneath a cloud.

"I have my own demons to exorcise, my friend. Thank you for sharing your story. It's fascinating. Thank you for this wonderful day together. And now I must leave you, but part of me will linger with you for quite a while. Aloha, dear friend." I kissed Sam on the cheek. Then I looked over my shoulder and saw the other man rapidly approaching.

"Aloha, Adrian," I said.

He unlocked the door to room 327 and swung it wide open.

"Come in, Suzanne. I've been looking forward to this all day." Adrian smiled and beamed charm as I brushed past him.

His room, larger than mine, featured one king-sized bed and pretty honey-colored furniture. A tall armoire stood between the bed and the sliding glass doors to the lanai.

205

Escape plan. I could always run onto the porch balcony and make a fuss if Adrian tried anything.

"Did you enjoy your day seeing the island?" he asked.

"Oh, yes. It was most enjoyable. I feel very much at home here."

"I've done this conference several times here on Kauai and I have yet to see much of the island. You'd think that I would allow a few extra days for sightseeing."

"Maybe your wife and children could join you," I said innocently.

"Yes, well, we'd better get started. There isn't a good induction chair in this room. I like to use a lounger, something that's comfortable. We have these wooden chairs," he said, pointing to two chairs by a small round table near the sliding glass doors, "or you could relax back on the bed if you want. I really think the bed might be more comfortable for you." A pink candle in a glass votive holder burned on the table, its odor sweet like plumerias.

"A chair will do just fine," I said quickly. "I might just fall asleep on the bed." *You pervert. I must get my attitude adjusted.*

He gestured to the chair after pulling it to the center of the room. I sat down and made myself comfortable while he dimmed the lights, leaving the lamp on at his bedside table. He sat down in the other chair, pulled near me, and spoke in a calm, grounded voice.

"I want you to get comfortable now, Suzanne, in your chair with your legs and feet relaxed, your head and arms releasing all tension."

I couldn't resist and interrupted him, saying, "Aren't you going to dangle a pocket watch in front of my eyes?"

"That's not been in vogue for decades. I'm sure you've done many regressions yourself as a psychologist. But if you like, I could dig out a quartz pendulum from somewhere." He sounded testy, not at all amused.

"I was just teasing you. I'll behave myself now and won't interrupt any more. Maybe I'm just anxious about the regression. Sometimes the information can be unsettling." I shifted in the chair with its padded seat.

"It's all right, Suzanne. I can bring you out at any moment. You can signal me by raising your right hand. I'm glad you interrupted me because I neglected to ask if there's a particular lifetime you are examining. You may have told me, but I can't recall. I can't always guarantee we'll end up there, but at least I can try to shift us in that direction."

"Yes, absolutely. I'm looking at a past life in the early 1940's. I don't know what my name was, but I was a woman with long blonde hair who sang with a swing band and lived in a Victorian house. One scrying episode showed this woman lying dead in the woods. I'm trying to figure out what happened to her."

"I see." Adrian held his chin in one hand. "I may very well help you see what you need to know. It must be important information for you."

I settled back and breathed deeply into my abdomen to unwind.

"I want you to relax completely in every part of your body. Relax your head, face ..." Adrian started at my crown and named all the parts of my body. He spoke softly, nearly in a monotone.

"Now imagine you're on a beach, the sun blazing down upon you. You are even more relaxed, and then a breeze cools you off. You feel soothed, relaxed, your body limp.

"Now listen carefully as I count down and know with every number you will become increasingly relaxed: ten—your neck and shoulders are melting, the muscles releasing all tension and cares, nine—your arms and hands feel soothing energies shooting into them, releasing every last muscle to glorious relaxation..." Adrian continued until he reached one. Then he talked about a golden staircase and counted down from five to one as I descended the staircase and became even more relaxed.

"Finally, you have entered a large, circular room. In the center of the room is a full-length mirror. Go to it and look at yourself. See yourself the way you look today.

"You look beautiful, Suzanne, with your porcelain features and dark flowing hair. But watch as the image begins to blur and you see an image of yourself from long ago, another lifetime. You are also a woman, very pretty, with long, blonde hair who lived in a Victorian house and sang and danced during the Big Band era. Tell me, who do you see in the mirror now?"

"It's me," I said simply.

"What's your name?"

"Elene Page."

"Tell me, Elene Page, tell me what you are seeing," he said in his soft, deep, hypnotic voice.

I heard his words and knew I was in the room with him.

Yet I was also in this other place as I stepped into the Victorian house I had seen in my crystal ball. I was walking down the stairs wearing a purple dress and red slippers. I could see my blonde hair falling about my face.

I put my hand against my chest and stopped. The sensation of dread was oddly familiar.

"Where are you?" he asked, intruding on my vision.

"I'm on the stairs of my house and I'm caught by some dark emotions—mostly dread and fear. My lover's coming to take me away, and I am torn about leaving my husband."

"Perhaps you love this new man and not your husband any longer?" he suggested.

"No. That isn't it at all. I can barely stand Victor, my agent. He's a weak, ordinary sort of man, but he appeals to my dreams. He says he can make me famous, that I'll be singing all over the world. I long for a life beyond this one in

Pittsburgh. I want to be famous; I want to be adored by many." My voice sounded tinny, like someone else's.

"Do you believe this will happen, that you will become famous, Elene?"

I clasped my hands and grew tense. "Oh, I don't know. I don't know what I believe any more. I doubt that it would make me happy. But I have to shoot for it. I can't stay here. I've gone too far already. Michael has begun to suspect the changes in me."

"Michael?"

"He's my husband. He's been good to me, loving and supportive. He helped me get my first singing gig.

"But listen, sir, I must get ready. Victor's coming. I have to leave a letter for Michael to try and explain all this. I don't think he will understand, but I don't want to cut myself off from him forever. He may want me back, after I'm rich and famous. Just maybe we could get back together again. I certainly don't want to spend much time with this Victor guy." I sat shivering in the chair.

"Please excuse me while I write my letter," I said, and in my mind, the vision continued.

Chapter Twenty

I sat at the dark wood dining room table in my purple dress and wrote on a pale cream sheet of paper. My hands were smaller, more delicate-looking than now. A few tears splatted haphazardly onto the paper.

After the longest time, I blotted up the tears with a handkerchief, blew on the paper to dry them, folded and stuffed the paper into an envelope, and set it in the center of the table. I turned my head as I heard noise out back.

"What is going on, Elene?" Adrian asked me.

"I heard rattling at the back door. Since Victor doesn't have a key to the house, I realized it must be Michael. I grabbed the letter and raced up the stairs, heart pounding, looking for a hiding place. My dresser. I pulled one of the small drawers completely out, stashed the letter behind it, and shoved it back in, quick and quiet as I could be.

"Hoping I could get rid of Michael before Victor came, I walked back down the stairs, trying to look casual and not a nervous wreck. It was moving too fast now, and I couldn't be sure of what was happening.

"I didn't hear Michael's car out back, so he must have parked and walked in. What did that mean? Does he know what's going on? Why come home two hours early? Surely he must suspect something is wrong. Unlike today, Michael has always been perfectly predictable in the past.

"He met me at the bottom of the stairs and hugged me soundly. It put me off my guard entirely, and I almost forgot about the whole scenario unfolding in my life.

"'Michael,' I said, not wanting to appear overly anxious or out of character, either, 'What are you doing home? And where's your car?'

"'Elene,' he said, 'you've been on my mind constantly. I can't get you out. You're my wife and I don't want to lose you. I can't describe exactly what I've been feeling, but it's as if you're slipping away from me by inches. I can't ignore it anymore.'

"'But why couldn't you say that when you came home tonight?' This was taking too long.

"'I felt like something was happening. I almost expected some other guy to be here with you, Elene. I'm sorry I'm not trusting you, but you haven't been with me lately. You've been miles away.'

"'I'm sorry, Michael, I really am.' I searched in my mind for a way out of this dilemma. Victor would be here any minute now. 'Let's go somewhere and talk about this. I've been cooped up in the house all day.' My packed bag was on our bed upstairs. I couldn't explain that to Michael, either.

"'Why do you want to leave the house, Elene? We'll have more privacy here. What's going on?'

"Just as I opened my mouth to speak, I heard his car pull up out back, the engine noisy from some kind of exhaust leak. I didn't know what to do, but I felt a strong urge to escape. I swallowed and held fast, for Michael could run faster than me.

"He was at the back door, knocking. I was frozen, rooted at the bottom of the stairs. Somehow, I never dreamed this could happen. Michael strode over and wrenched open the door. Victor's face said it all. He looked from Michael to me, looking for some explanation.

"'What are you doing here?' Michael said, hatred marring his features.

"'I'll just be going,' Victor said. 'You seem busy, Elene. I'll come back another day.' He gingerly backed himself away from the doorway.

"'You get back here,' Michael growled. He grabbed Victor by the arm and yanked him into the room.

"'Now listen here. I just came to talk to your wife. I have business dealings with her. I can be a big boost to her career. She needs an agent.'

"'I don't believe you, you slime. I saw you once at a dance, gawking at her like a kid drooling over candy. You have some other kind of deal in mind. You just sit there,' Michael said, roughly shoving Victor into an armchair.

"I had never seen Michael so incensed. It was as if he had become a wild animal defending his territory. I didn't even feel as if this new, enraged Michael loved me. I was an object—his object—and he was establishing ownership.

213

"'Michael,' I said, slumping into another armchair. 'Victor's right. He's been talking to me, offering to be my agent. You know how much the singing career means to me. I really don't have much of a chance without an agent.'

"'Right. So why is he coming to our house in the middle of the day while I'm working? Why haven't you told me about this agent deal before? You're leaving out a few details. This isn't hard to figure out.' Michael's hand was on my upper arm; in his frenzy, his fingers tightened until I winced from pain.

"'That hurts, Michael,' I said, and he released me. He paced in the room.

"'I don't know what to do about this. I just don't know what to do,' he said, then he catapulted up the stairs. I knew he kept a loaded gun near the bed, the bed beneath my packed suitcase.

"'Run,' I said to Victor, who had already bolted from his chair, sweat dripping from his face. He never turned around, nor offered to take me with him, just vanished out the back door. I heard the engine roar, tires screeching, and I knew I would never see Victor again.

"I stood trembling, wondering why I hadn't run, too. I could hear him crashing down the stairs and ..." I paused.

"What is it? What's happening, Elene?" Adrian Stein's voice came from far away.

"She's gone," I whispered. "Elene has gone. I can't see any more. I'm not there in the Victorian any more. I'm here with you again."

Adrian spoke briefly to help me make the transition back to Kauai, but it wasn't necessary. I had left the horrible scene. Somehow my mind had blocked out the events that followed it.

"Adrian, I need the rest. I can't understand why it stopped just now."

"Your mind had gotten enough information for this session. We would have to do another regression to try to delve further, and there's no guarantee we would even return to that lifetime or continue on with the story." Adrian was holding my hands, his touch reassuring.

"I was going to make a few post hypnotic suggestions, but you've come back too fast," Adrian mumbled.

"What suggestions?"

"Oh, so you'd show me some affection, that sort of thing."

I couldn't believe he was telling me this. "It wouldn't have worked anyway, Adrian. You should know that."

"I like a challenge, Suzanne, and you've been one. And occasionally I'm surprised and the post hypnotic work yields results. I was anxious to try it on you."

"So you're really not concerned about helping me with my past life dilemma. It's more like a sexual conquest thing." I tried to not sound irritated with him, for I'd already suspected his motives.

"But I am trying to help you. Even after all these years I find the past life information fascinating. I'm always in need of fresh information, and the variety of it boggles my mind."

"So you're not in it to help me," I reiterated. "It's for your research."

He looked utterly exasperated, and he stood, releasing my hands.

"I'm not such a bad guy, you know, Suzanne. I'm not such a bad guy after all. I do lots of good in this world, whatever my motives. I usually get paid for this type of work, and paid well, so I guess my motive is money, but that's why most people work."

"I don't know why I'm being so hard on you, Adrian. Please forgive me. You've been very kind to work with me, and I've made such progress. I would be more than happy to pay you for the regression." Adrian had brought me to the brink of the information I sought, and I did feel grateful to him, also disappointed in myself and my attitude.

"Oh, I've plenty of money. It'll just go for alimony and child support, anyway. Why don't we just get comfortable and watch some television?" Adrian motioned toward the king-size bed instead of the TV set. I choked back an urge to laugh out loud.

"I guess I'd better go back to my room and get ready for tomorrow. With the jet lag and all, I go to sleep with the chickens on this island." Besides, I needed to think about Elene and Michael.

"Want to do another regression tomorrow night?"

I thought about those post hypnotic suggestions and my poor attitude and decided I didn't want to push on further, though the next session with this talented man could tell me all I needed to know. After all, was he using me or was I using him?

"No, thank you, though you've helped me so much already. Thank you for sharing your gift of hypnotic regression. I think I'd better process this information before I try to delve in further. This piece has been traumatic. I'll let it rest so that the next information might come more easily. I never expected anything like this dramatic story when I bought my crystal ball."

"I understand. I'm here if you change your mind. Want me to walk you to your room?"

I smiled and shook his hand. "No, Adrian. There are plenty of ladies here at the conference, aching to throw themselves at you. I'm a waste of time, so good night, dear doctor."

"Maybe I enjoy having my time wasted," he mumbled as I turned with a wave and escaped to the hallway.

The air in the hallway surrounded me, fresh and clean, and I inhaled great gulps of the stuff, suddenly yearning for the sanctity of my room, a cup of aromatic hot tea, and space to meditate.

Early the next morning, the phone rang exactly twice before I heard him pick up.

"James?" I said.

"Hello, Jim's dog watching service. Have you a canine in need of walking, feeding, and pampering?"

I giggled. James was never boring.

"Hello, Suzanne. What time is it there? It's a little after noon here. I take it you're still across the ocean there beneath a palm tree."

"It's six a.m. here. I just woke up and decided to try you. It was too late to call last night. And there are no palm trees in my room, but I can see acres of them outside the window. I have a lanai, you know."

"I know. That's one of those outrigger canoe thingies, isn't it? And you just called to say you missed me."

"Of course I miss you, and I was wondering about Princess and how she's doing."

"She's doing fine. I have her here over at my house most of the time. Do you want to talk to her?"

I could hear James saying, "Speak, speak!" in the background. Finally, I heard her familiar "woof!" in response. In my mind I envisioned her shaggy furred body and trusting brown eyes, and I smiled and was reassured.

"She said she misses you," James said.

"And she's been good on her walks and she's eating all right?" My mothering instincts had kicked in.

"Yes, Suzanne, don't worry. She's eating fine—first thing in the morning, a whole bowl of dog chow. She's been walking me all over Crafton. I've never been in better shape."

"Thank you, James. I knew you'd do a great job, but I can't help but worry about her. It's really silly."

"So what's going on there in coconut land? Tough to get the lanai out past the surf?"

"It's a porch—lanai means porch. To answer your first question, the conference is interesting, and a psychologist who's a native here took me on a tour of the island. I'm having a great time, especially with you watching Princess."

"So you have an island boyfriend?" James's interest sounded casual, maybe too casual.

"No, nothing like that. He's just a friend. I'm here to relax, James; that boy-girl stuff can be brutal."

"Everything's fine here. So just enjoy yourself there in paradise."

"I'd better go. Got to slurp down some heavenly pineapple, walk the beach, study the sun and clouds, and make the best of
it before the next class starts."

"You learning anything about your past lives?" he asked as an afterthought.

"No, not really. It's a fascinating subject, though. Maybe I'll practice on you when I get back." As was my policy, I chose not to share my discoveries with Adrian.

"I'm not much of a guinea pig, but maybe you could work on Princess. Maybe she was an ancient Egyptian princess and that's why you named her that."

"All right, James, and thank you again for your expert care of the royal dog, but I'll go now. Aloha."

Hearing Princess's woofs made me homesick for her, yet our conversation also kicked up uneasy vibes about going home. I almost wished I hadn't called, for the reality of returning to my life back across the waters was oddly disturbing. So I bolted out of bed, threw on my shorts outfit, and prepared to immerse myself in another day in paradise. If I ran really fast on the beach, I might leave my past behind forever.

Chapter Twenty-One

I could hardly believe my week on Kauai was nearly done. Tonight was my final evening to enjoy soothing island breezes, to marvel at the tropical foliage, to listen to the roosters crow (chickens ran wild all over the island). Tomorrow I would drive back to Lihue airport for the short hop to Oahu, then to Atlanta, then home.

If it weren't for Princess, I might just stay here. The thought was tempting.

I dressed in the sleeveless tropical flowered blue dress I'd bought at the Coconut Marketplace. The dark and lighter blue fabric looked rich, and as a bonus, the short skirt swirled as I turned. I slipped a dolphin earring in shiny sterling silver into each earlobe and admired for the tenth time my aquamarine white gold pendant.

Though I dressed with great care and attention to detail tonight, I assured myself that I wasn't making any fuss over my appearance. As I grabbed my hairbrush and arranged my hair for the third time, I started to laugh.

"You really are being ridiculous," I told the smiling girl who might have passed as an island woman with her tan skin and long, full, fluffy dark hair.

I met Sam in the lobby of the hotel, walking off the elevator just as he stepped inside. I chuckled and we smiled at each other as old friends do.

"Are you ready for one last evening on the garden isle?" Sam asked, looking native as ever in his red floral print shirt and white pants.

"I think I'm ready to tear up the plane ticket and stay here," I said.

"That could be arranged, my dear." He flattered me with one of his piercing gazes. "Shall we go?"

Before I could answer, Adrian Stein brushed past us with a nod of his head, a statuesque redhead with perfect features on his arm. She appeared to be talking nonstop, and I imagined that I saw a slightly pained expression on his face.

"That the lady who's getting all the past life regressions now?" Sam asked after they had sufficiently passed beyond us.

"He didn't make any more offers to me after he immediately latched on to her. Or maybe she latched on to him. It's starting to look that way." I giggled. "I hope she's incredibly boring. Anyway, to answer your question, I don't think they're doing past life regressions. I think their work together is more in the present life area."

"So enough of this Adrian Stein guy. We've already had to listen to him for days on end. Putting him aside—far aside— shall we head out for some island adventure?"

"You're the tour guide, Sam. I'm up for almost anything."

He raised his eyebrows. "Night tour of the Kalalau Trail? I've got a torch in the trunk."

"No, thank you. I could barely navigate those boulders during daylight. I'm up for almost anything else."

"Plan B, then. We're headed west, young lady, for parts unknown. You look nice. That's an understatement—you look gorgeous, Suzanne." He took my hand and twirled me around.

"Thank you, kind sir. And if we were on the Emy Jo again, I'd have to fight off all the other ladies."

He escorted me through the parking lot past the blossoming bushes and trees. The late afternoon sun shone golden over all, giving the island a rich coating. The air felt silken, the hours ahead incredibly promising. I reached to the ground and picked up a creamy plumeria blossom with its heavy petals, inhaling deeply of its sweetness.

"Right here, Miss," Sam said as we approached his black Jeep Wrangler.

I slid the flower behind my ear, then stepped into the passenger seat. Sam already sat behind the wheel and started the engine. The convertible top was down on the Jeep, so I pulled my hair back.

As he wheeled us out of the parking lot onto a small road that turned onto the main road, I experienced an exhilaration that I couldn't remember feeling back in Pittsburgh.

Another perfect moment in a perfect place, and I never felt so alive. Here I was riding with an intelligent, attractive man, going somewhere, I didn't even know where, on the brink of another adventure.

We rode in silence for miles along the two-lane road that skirted the coast. There were few roads inland, for Mt. Waialeale rose in the middle of Kauai, always covered by clouds, the wettest spot on earth.

I could see peninsulas of land sticking out, golden flashes of beaches, distant houses and structures. We wheeled past the airport, and a knot formed in my throat. That would be tomorrow—this was tonight.

On we drove past sugar cane, the red dirt decorating the fields. We briefly passed through a tunnel of tall eucalyptus trees.

"This looked better before the last hurricane," Sam said as he turned around and drove us back through the trees again. "This was just a side show, not our destination. Can't let you miss anything."

As we drove further and further west, I finally remembered from my map reading and studying of guide books what lay on the west of Kauai.

"Sam, I think I know where we're going."

"And?"

"I think we're headed for Polihale State Park to watch the sunset." I hated to spoil his surprise, but the destination excited me. "What fun!"

"You've read the guidebooks."

"It was a tourist newspaper."

"Yes, my pretty wahine, for this one last evening, we watch the sunset. With your psychological cunning you have deduced our destination. But you still haven't seen it, and that's the best part."

As he drove up the west, the road turned to dirt, but was navigable, but barely at points. Huge holes and ruts in the road forced us to crawl so that the last mile or so of road stretched for an eternity. We passed just a few other vehicles, mostly of the four-wheel variety. This track afforded no view of the ocean, so I just trusted it was ahead. When we came to the end of the road at last, Sam parked. We saw only a few red and white rental cars parked here, with a few others belonging to locals. (The rentals came in either red or white, which had become a joke with me. Why only red and white?)

"Come, pretty lady. Island boy will celebrate with you the end of this beautiful day, the end of this beautiful week, and it looks like the end of this beautiful friendship."

Sadness settled around me, like a heavy, drab spirit. I looked across at him as we walked a pathway to the beach, sand sifting into my white sandals.

"Sam," I said softly, "it has been a beautiful week. But our friendship will never end. Even if I never see you again or hear from you, you will be in my heart. You'll always be a part of me, like this beautiful island."

"I'll miss you, Suzanne. Didn't mean to get so serious. It's just that our time together has been so comfortable and I hate for it to end."

225

"Same here, my friend. Perhaps we've become such good friends because we knew it would be for a limited time only, and because we've stayed within the boundaries of friendship."

We sighted the beach, with its wide expanse of sand and rolling waves, where just a few couples lingered. We walked up, away from the others to a secluded spot. Sam threw down a soft, plaid blanket he'd brought from the Jeep and we settled upon it, kicking off our sandals. A few kids were trying to surfboard, and we watched in amusement.

"It's the best place on the island to watch the sunset," he confided.

"That's what the tourist newspaper said. Are you a reporter for that publication?"

"Just a humble native."

"Have you ever thought of leaving this island?" I asked as I pulled my dress down to a respectable spot above my knees.

"I did leave, when I went to school and took my psychology training. I was gone for several years. I even thought of locating in San Francisco after I completed my degree."

"What brought you back?"

"I told myself it was my wife. But that wasn't it, after all, for now she's gone and I'm still firmly grounded in this place. And I have no thoughts of leaving.

"I'd say the island gets in your blood, and there's a peace and contentment I can find no other place on earth. So I guess I just belong here—like this beach."

"And all the other Ho brothers," I said as the sky and sea melded together in color. "I envy you, Sam. I'd love to live here. This island speaks to me as a special, holy place."

We talked quietly, often laughing, as the sun became a ball of fluorescent orange-red color sinking into the sea. We lingered even as the darkness crept out, obscuring the lines of the land, sea, and sky.

He stood and reached for my hand. A spot warmed my shoulder where I had been leaning against him. He pulled me up, and for just a moment I thought we would embrace, but instead we shook out the plaid blanket and folded it. Just one, tiny awkward moment, and my disappointment surprised me.

"Want to get something to eat?" he asked as we strolled to the Jeep.

"Yes, I guess the sea air's making me hungry," I said brightly.

"The last supper," he said soberly.

"I can see the missionaries got to you." I was recovering now.

"Worse than that. My father is a minister, retired now."

He drove us back toward the south, finding an inn near the beach. We entered and were ushered through tables with flickering oil lamps; dark Tiki gods set the décor, as well as red tablecloths. The hostess showed us outside to an open air area where there were fewer Tiki gods, but the evening breezes fanned us. The restaurant looked about half filled.

I ordered the mahi mahi, perfectly cooked so that it melted in my mouth, and he ate steak, and we talked about inconsequential things for the most part, a steady banter that made me smile and wish for more nights like this one. We were well into our entrees when the mood shifted.

"I've scried about you and me, Suzanne, because I feel so close to you. The results were interesting," Sam said as he buttered a roll. The oil lamp flickered and cast light shapes on his face as if we were sitting at a tribal circle.

"That's funny, I came up with a past life experience with you and me, too, during one of our group regressions at the seminar. Who'd have thought Adrian Stein would bring us together?" Another reason to be grateful to Adrian, I noted.

"What's your story?" he asked.

"Your turn first. You brought it up."

He grinned, and his teeth were white and even.

"All right, my contrary wahine friend. I'll talk first. Mine is a pretty story, certainly not dramatic or filled with conflict, but interesting, nonetheless.

"It was you and me together, right from the beginning and throughout our lives. We grew up on one of these islands; I'm not sure which one. We were brother and sister—you the brother, I the sister—and we grew up sturdy and brown. Our parents had no other children, and we didn't live near other people. You and I played together and were happy.

"When the time came to leave our family and make our own lives, we built a hut not far from our parents and lived together there. We were content with a simple life with few other companions, living close to nature. It wasn't a sexual relationship then, either." He paused and took a sip of coffee.

"And when we were old, we were a great comfort to each other, always being there, attending to the other's needs," I said, picking up the thread of the story. My excitement grew by the minute. "And I think I know how we died."

"You do?" Sam raised his eyebrows.

"There was a huge storm and we went to look for pigs that had gotten loose. We went together and were standing near the shore when a gigantic wave carried us out to sea."

"How did you know that?" Sam asked. "This is my story."

I ignored his protests. "My last sensation was of joy and happiness as we were being carried away. It was as if my spirit had lifted from my body and I didn't suffer or feel anything bad."

"You got the same story," he said, eyes wide.

"Looks that way. So there must be something to it. It must be real."

As we finished our meal, I admired him—his looks and personality—and had thoughts that were not sisterly. Maybe it was fortunate I was leaving in the morning. I knew I couldn't keep cool and proper much longer.

When we arrived back at the Coconut Beach Hotel, he parked and walked me up the sloping drive to the hotel lobby.

229

"I can take you to the airport tomorrow," he said, and I knew he meant it.

"I appreciate your offer, but I turn in my rental car at the airport. I think I'd rather say goodbye tonight, brother."

"Just be sure when you get to your room you lock the door tight and don't even answer it if anyone knocks. That Adrian Stein might make one last ditch effort to seduce you. I don't think the red-haired woman worked out to his liking."

"Yes, brother."

"And you can call me anytime you want, write me, whatever. Put my address and phone number in your book as soon as you get home. And let me know about this past lifetime murder stuff. I'll help in any way I can. I am concerned about your safety."

"I'll let you know what happens. You're sweet to worry about me. And you can call me anytime, too, or write or email. Or even come to visit in Pittsburgh." I was starting to choke up, holding the grief safely in place. We wouldn't keep in touch. Nobody ever did. They were just words, and we'd probably forget each other in time.

"So goodbye for now," he said and embraced me very tenderly. Time and space disappeared, and a gentleness suffused into me. He comforted me as he always did and had in our past life.

"I won't forget you, Sam," I said and watched as he turned to go. He had walked halfway to the Jeep when he stopped in his tracks and turned around. He ran back to me and grabbed me with such force that we whirled around.

"You are not my sister in this lifetime, Suzanne, and I won't let you go without this." This time the embrace sent bolts of energy throughout my entire body, and as he kissed me white hot energies erupted up my spine. Something within shifted.

I felt light-headed as he let me go. Dizzy and blissful.

"Perhaps we will meet again in this lifetime, brother who is certainly not my brother, thank heavens."

"I would like that, wahine of my heart."

Chapter Twenty-Two

I sat slumped at the kitchen table meditating on a sugar loaf pineapple, my green suitcase and purple and black carryon bag tossed around me. My green Bermuda shorts were comfortable, and only slightly wrinkled from the long flights. I'd worn my gray fleece jacket over my white eyelet sleeveless top to adjust for the temperature difference.

I had just arrived home.

The flights had been uneventful and on time, with no surprises of the grit-your- teeth kind. At the Oahu airport I had eaten a light meal at a fast food place whose windows opened onto a delightful oriental garden, complete with flashing orange fish and pagodas.

The flight from Oahu was brightened by a ten-year-old pink beribboned girl with long blonde hair from Atlanta who chattered away and made the hours pass quickly. I couldn't recall much about the flight from Atlanta to Pittsburgh, except that we were in the air only an hour.

Sandy met me at the airport, all bright and excited about my trip, and dropped me off in Crafton. For once, I couldn't keep up my end of the conversation. I apologized for my jet-lagged condition and promised to call her soon. She said she expected a blow by blow account of my travels, complete with pictures, maybe with a crystal ball reading thrown in.

And now, more than ever, in the silence of my home, I didn't want to be here. The dread returned, and I again faced an uncertain future, not knowing what lay ahead or where peril might sideswipe me. I was safe on Kauai, far removed from this drama, in spite of Adrian's past life regression. But here I could feel my stomach knotting up already.

The house echoed with emptiness—no Princess. It was amazing how her presence filled all the corners and nooks of this big place.

I glanced at my watch: eleven a.m. Pittsburgh time. James must have Princess next door at his place. I wanted to go get her, but my dull, heavy body protested. I hadn't slept in nearly twenty-four hours.

And here I was home to a brewing storm in my life and not a palm tree anywhere in sight. How would I ever survive here?

My mail was stacked neatly on the table, but it held no appeal in my groggy state. I decided to check my answering machine.

I abandoned the luggage, considering it too heavy to lug upstairs in my weakened state, and stepped surprisingly lightly to the upper landing. I entered my bedroom, a hollowness ringing there, and it looked spacious and clean. The sun beamed through lead crystal ornaments hanging in my windows, making little rainbows on the walls, and I

233

remembered the many rainbows of Hawaii. This must be a Pennsylvania aloha welcome home. The bed invited me, and

I nearly succumbed, but my strategy was to stay up today to beat jet lag and crash a little early tonight.

The dresser caught my attention. I had waited a long time for this opportunity. Ever since my regression with Adrian, I'd itched to search for the letter Elene had written to Michael. I pulled out the small drawer at the top right and set it on the bed. I stooped and peered into the dark space. Surely enough, a yellowed envelope was wedged at the back.

With trembling hands, I carefully removed the letter, which rested across my palms. Somehow, this didn't seem possible. I stared at the envelope, upon which "Michael" was written in round, almost childlike lettering.

It didn't look anything like my handwriting.

Could this really be a letter I'd written to my husband years ago? I slid the letter out, the paper discolored and friable, and placed the envelope and myself on the bed.

Opening the ivory sheet carefully, I wondered if the words I'd written many years ago would sound familiar. With pounding heart, I read:

Dear Michael,

As you know, I have loved you for many years. You were all I wanted and all I lived for. When we learned we could never have children, we were there for each other, and our love pulled us through that rough time as well as every other tough spot.

These past several years have been different, though. We have drifted apart. You have been so busy, and we hardly laugh together any more. I'm feeling lost and confused, and I'd love to have our old life back.

If you remember, you were the one who encouraged me in my singing career. Maybe you just wanted me to stop begging you for attention, for a little time together. You wanted me to sing, and I grew to love my career.

Then the singing began to take over, and I thought of little else. I dreamed of becoming a big star, of traveling around the country, even the world. My fantasy world became more real than the real world, and all I wanted was to dream of my new life as a famous singer.

That's when Victor came to town. He spoke to me after I'd sung at a swing dance. I wasn't deceived by him—he's a shallow person and uses everyone he touches—but I believed his words. I was so desperate for attention that I became involved with him. You must not blame me for this, Michael, for I have begged you for help, and you refused me every time.

I do not love Victor. Many times I don't even like him. That is the truly sad part, my beloved Michael. I still have all the old feelings for you, and I long only for you, but I cannot have you.

Lately, I've had disturbing dreams. Remember the other morning when I was shaking and crying and you held me, but I said I couldn't remember?

I did remember, but couldn't tell you. I was in a wooded area, walking around the woods near our house. I could see someone lying on the ground, so I rushed over to help the person. When I got there, I couldn't believe my eyes.

The person on the ground was me, and I was dead.

I've dreamed of hands choking me, wringing the life from me. When I woke up, I was sweating, and I could swear the hands were yours, Michael.

I fear for my life, Michael, and I fear you, whom I have loved most in this world. So I am going away with Victor. I don't believe I can discuss this with you. The time for discussion is far behind us.

I don't want Victor. I don't want a life with him, or to spend my days and nights with him.

I only want you.

And so I go. Perhaps in future years we can be together again. Maybe later you'll understand and choose to be with me again.

Please don't try to find me.

Love,
Elene

I held the pages to my chest, not at all surprised by my discovery. I'd been sure that she loved Michael and now I understood her interest in Victor.

But to read these words that I had written in another lifetime, to touch the very paper I had touched before—eerie sensations enveloped me.

I glanced over at the black silk scarf on my bedside table. With a sense of urgency, I uncovered the quartz sphere, the light striking colors within it. I carefully carried it to my desk, placing Elene's letter in my desk drawer. The sphere drew me as never before, and I prayed the answers would now be revealed.

I breathed deeply, slowly, and eased into the crystal, waiting for the story to unfold. I thought: *Elene and Michael,*

236

Elene and Michael, their final scene together. I didn't expect, yet I hoped and waited.

Clouds rolled through, then the sphere became clear, crystal clear, and it was as if I were in that hotel room with Adrian Stein again. The curtain had lifted, and Elene appeared again, just as my regression had left her, trembling, fearful, even becoming frantic.

Michael came crashing down the stairs. He didn't carry the shotgun, and for a moment I felt relief for Elene. Silly, I knew how the story ended.

He held her packed suitcase in one hand and raised it and shook it as he raged at her. His features contorted and were made evil by his emotion, the veins of his neck standing out in his maniacal state of mind.

Her eyes grew wide and she opened her mouth to speak, but he pushed at her with one powerful hand. Then he gave the suitcase a wild toss and it landed heavily, but didn't open.

Elene started to run, as if finally realizing she must escape, but he grabbed her, both hands closing around her neck, and shook her forcefully.

He fumed at her and shook, her head bobbing almost gracefully, her arms, which had at first pulled at him, as if to plead for mercy, fell to her sides.

I could sense the life oozing out of her, saw her slipping away until she hovered above the scene and watched even as I watched from below. Long after she had left the body, he continued to rage at her. When he stopped, he suddenly noticed her limpness, and his face transformed as if he changed masks to one of utter horror.

She fell flaccid upon the dining room floor and he knelt beside her, cradling her in his arms and crying.

Much later, he sat in a chair and stared, long after it had grown dark, and then he left the house and brought the car back. He gathered her into his arms, kissing her tenderly before taking her out, and carefully deposited her in the back seat of the car.

He drove for what seemed like many hours, until he reached a remote forested area. The car rattled and shook as he guided it on dirt tracks as far back as he could manage. Finally, he parked and carried her into the woods, hiking and stumbling, occasionally stopping to cry helplessly. At last he placed her on the ground and arranged her there, as if she were a sleeping maiden waiting for the handsome prince.

His plan, or lack of one, left little thought or hope for success. He drove off in the car, and I wondered if he would run away or go back home to the empty house.

The sphere cleared again, and I was back here in my bedroom, just returned from my lovely trip to Kauai.

At last, I'd witnessed the final scene of Elene Page, and the story was neither complex nor particularly original. She'd been a victim of her time, when women didn't have their own lives, when their dreams largely were unrecognized and ignored.

She and her husband had not communicated their small griefs until it all came to one large grief, which could have been avoided. Why was it that I couldn't muster up any ill will toward Elene or Michael? They were victims of their own private agendas, and of the rotten wind that had blown through their lives known as Victor.

Victor had been the catalyst that had catapulted the situation from moderately unhappy to deadly. He must not have even called the police to try to help her. He must have blown back from wherever he came.

I sat for the longest time, trying to digest all this. I sat until I figured that I must get on with my life in the here and now. I must not become too caught up in the past.

Yet one fact penetrated my dull thinking processes: I knew the entire story, but I still didn't know where danger lurked for me now. Who would try to kill me? The urge to cry nearly overcame me as I considered just giving up.

The blinking light on the answering machine caught my attention, the number flashing "5." Only five messages at home in my week-long absence. Unsure whether to be upset or joyful, I decided five messages were plenty enough. Besides, I didn't feel like answering them now.

I touched the play button, and a lady from the Crafton library announced that my Mary Stewart book, *This Rough Magic*, had come in. I sincerely hoped I could pick it up before it was due back in. Besides that, I wasn't sure if I needed to read an adventure-mystery-romance book. My life of late was the makings of one.

His voice filled the room and a chill raced up along my spine. I listened carefully as he said in his message: "Suzanne, I've missed you. I have an urgent need to meet with you. I know I have an appointment with you on Friday, but could I please see you as soon as you get back? This is Brad."

Brad. I had almost forgotten about him. But I didn't even want to be here in this land without palms swaying in the breezes. I didn't want to handle any serious problems. And I wasn't sure that I could help Brad with his rages, especially since he targeted women.

I hadn't expected to hear the voice on the next message, and it gave me a little jump: "Listen, doll, I know we haven't been seeing each other, but I'm getting a little lonely here—for you, that is. I was wondering if you might want to get together, listen to some music, go dancing, have some laughs. You know who this is. Give me a call."

Now a fine tremor shook throughout my body. I could visualize scenes from my past lifetime: the one in the dining room with Elene and Victor, the final tragic scene with Elene and Michael. My heart sped up, and with effort, I commanded myself to take slow, deep breaths.

Mike had called. And I had decided I wouldn't see him again. Did I need to see him once more to unravel the secrets of the past? Or would that be a fatal mistake?

My first impulse was to run and toss the answering machine into Chartiers Creek. I guess that answered my question.

With growing reservations, I listened on. I shouldn't have worried, for the voice was familiar and non-threatening. "Suzanne, this is Adrian. I just wanted to thank you for coming to the conference. You brightened up my days there, and I enjoyed working with you in the past life regression. If you want to try another regression or get in touch with me, you can call me at my office. The number is 415-555-2233. I'm often flitting around the country and would love to meet you somewhere. Hope all your regressions are happy ones. Bye now."

Once again, I paused between messages to collect myself and get the full impact of the message. I wanted to laugh out loud, but was too tired. So Adrian hadn't given up completely yet. He must know from experience what worked and what didn't with his conference women. I admired his persistence.

I paused before starting the final message, expecting some dramatic piece after hearing from Brad and Mike. My smile broke out as I heard his voice.

"Suzanne, there's a dog here who keeps mumbling your name. She's becoming very distraught. So if you'd like to retrieve your precious puppy, come on over to our house. Hope your trip went well. Aloha."

Silence. And in the silence of all the messages that hadn't been left, I noticed a lump in my throat.

Sam. There was no message from Sam Pahinui. I hadn't expected one, but I also hadn't expected to miss him this much. *If you fall for a guy, you have to pay the price.* But I'd tried so hard not to fall for him.

Jet lag. It was just travel weariness fogging up my brain. But why did I feel this ache like a smoldering coal in my heart?

I hadn't intended to return any calls. In fact, I had thought I'd run right over and get Princess and see James. But my training as a psychologist kicked in, and I automatically dialed Brad's phone number. I hoped he might be at work this time of day, and that I might get out of talking to him.

"Hello." I heard the deep voice that now only thrilled me in a negative way.

"Hi, Brad. This is Dr. Westin. I've just gotten back from my vacation, and I got your message. What's going on with you?"

"I really need to talk with you about something. Are you going to be there long?" he asked.

"I'm not seeing clients today. I'm still trying to get straightened up from jet lag. Could you just tell me about it over the phone?"

"Not really. It won't take long. I'll just stop over there and take a few minutes of your time."

"Not today. I'm not at the office. I'm not seeing clients." I heard a desperate note creeping into my speech.

"I know where you live," he said, and the line went dead.

Chapter Twenty-Three

By now, my return from paradise had a nightmarish quality to it, and I swore under my breath, wondering why I'd left such a gorgeous, safe island for this troubled place.

Was Brad a threat? Did he somehow fit into this past life drama? I quickly sorted through possibilities, also wondering if I should call the police.

But how could I call the police when I had nothing solid to base accusations on? Should I tell them I had been gazing in my crystal ball and knew I was in danger? Would I say I was Elene Page in a past life and murdered by her husband?

The phone rang and I jumped off the bed, nearly running into the wall. Too much was happening too fast for someone in my groggy condition.

"Hello," I said, dreading, yet hoping to hear Brad's deep voice. Maybe he couldn't find me.

"Hey, doll, I thought maybe something happened to you when I didn't hear from you," said the equally deep voice wafting out of the phone receiver.

"Mike?"

"The one and only."

"Just a minute." I put the receiver against my chest and tried to compose myself. An invisible iron hand clutched at my throat as my breathing became shallow.

"I want to go aloha," I mumbled as I replaced the receiver against my head.

"What was that?" Mike asked. I could picture him with his bald head and glasses, and he looked like Elene's Michael to the last detail. I don't think I had ever known true terror until this moment.

"Nothing, Mike. Listen, it's great of you to call, but I just got back from a trip and I can't talk right now."

"Where'd you go?" he asked.

"I can't talk now. One of my potentially violent clients has just called and is coming over here. I have to leave."

"Don't worry, Suzanne, I'll be right over."

I listened again to the monotonous chant of the dial tone.

Mike coming here, now?

I shivered and automatically moved out of the bedroom, down the hall, and down the stairway.

Why was I in danger? I was just a hard-working psychologist trying to help people. I hadn't harmed anyone as far as I knew.

Princess. Princess will protect me. I even called for her, expecting her to come racing from another room to save me, despite her gentle nature. Then I remembered I hadn't collected her yet, and another plan grew in my anxious mind.

I could hide out at James's until all the men who were coming after me had come and gone. Tomorrow, or in a day or two, when back in sync with this time and place, I would figure out what was happening to me.

Without further analysis, I raced next door, hoping James and Princess were home. If they weren't, I would have to disappear immediately in my car and maybe never come back.

I pounded at the back door and waited, with no results. I was making a quick dash to the front door, when the back door opened, and I heard James's voice.

"Is somebody out here?" James said, and Princess flew out the opened back door, flying right to me at the side of the house.

Our reunion touched me, and I'm not certain whose cries of welcome were more pitiful—Princess's or mine. She ran to me and as I held her, reassurance flooded my being.

"James, can you hide me? I'm fearing for my life right now and two guys I'm afraid of are coming right over and I can't be at my house." Princess licked my face as I spoke.

"Sure, come in. Stay as long as you like. Should I call the police?" He ushered Princess and me through the back door into the kitchen as he spoke, his face scrunched up in concern.

"No, I've nothing concrete to base this on. I'm just scared out of my wits." I sat at the kitchen table, my knees shaking.

"Why would they want to hurt you, Suzanne?" He sat down beside me.

"It's a long story and I'm not sure I understand any of it. The one guy has a history of rage directed toward women. It makes no sense at all."

"Would you like something to eat or drink? I guess you just got back from your trip."

"Yes, I just got home and I'm sorry I came back. Maybe some juice, if you have any."

"No problem." He opened the refrigerator, poured from a carafe, and returned with a jelly jar of orange-yellow fluid. I took it and sipped at citrus flavors gratefully as I petted Princess with long, soothing strokes that helped me more than they did her.

"Maybe we should go upstairs. I'm afraid they can see me in here." I was too close, after all. I should have escaped in my car, but it was too late now.

"We'll go up to my bedroom. We can see out back that way, but no one will be able to see us." James led me up the stairs into a bedroom best described as chaotic. There was even more clutter here than downstairs in the living room, a casual, bachelor residence.

"I don't think I've ever been up here before," I said, looking around. Princess had bounded up the stairs with me and was hugging my side.

"Have a seat," James said as he cleared off a chair covered with clothes near the bed.

My head started to pound, shifting my perspective. Why was I so paranoid? "This seems silly now. Maybe I should take Princess and go home."

"Stick around a while. You might as well stay here until the troops have gone. How was your trip?"

I filled him in on the highlights of my trip, leaving out any reference to Adrian Stein and the past life regressions. I did mention that the workshop leader was a womanizer.

"Did he give you extracurricular attention? Did you get an A+?" James asked.

"No, I found the whole idea just a little disgusting, especially since he has a wife and children. But the workshop was still fascinating."

James immediately became very chatty and told of his adventures with Princess in my absence. He had even taken her to the pet store where she found romance in the dog food aisle. A tiny, fluffy, white male dog and she had fallen instantly in love.

A glint of light across the room caught my eye. In this room of ultra-clutter, it was hard to see anything. I was surprised at my discovery.

"What is that over there, James?"

"Which thing do you mean? Order and tidiness are not exactly my specialties."

"A glass ball?"

"Oh, that." He rose from the bed and walked to the dresser and picked it up. "It's a crystal ball."

"Can I see it?"

"Sure." He handed it over, and I examined a quartz sphere larger and clearer than mine, a much higher quality scrying tool.

"This must have been pretty expensive," I said.

"I got a good deal on it. Did you pay a lot for yours?" he asked.

"How did you know I have one? I don't think I ever mentioned it." My stomach began to feel queasy.

"I had to follow Princess upstairs a few times while you were gone. I noticed it because I have one."

"Mine was covered." This was beginning to look suspicious, or was I being paranoid again?

"What else would you cover other than a crystal ball?" he said, though his sphere had been uncovered.

"What do you do with yours, James? Have you had it long?"

"I use it for scrying. I imagine you use yours for the same purpose. It's a little hobby of mine, just for fun. I bought my crystal ball long before you moved in next door. Am I right? Have you been crystal ball gazing?"

"Why, yes. I don't even know why I bought the thing. I'm not sure I'm glad I did. It hasn't been much fun lately. It's gotten way too serious."

"I'm not sorry. Sometimes the truth hurts. But the truth must be preserved above all costs," he said, his face closed and undecipherable.

"I've never seen you so serious before. This isn't anything like you." I said it lightly, but was beginning to feel alarmed.

"I'm hearing something down below. You stay here out of sight. Don't even try to peek. I'll check it out. Come on, Princess." She followed him out of the bedroom and plunked her way down the stairs.

He returned in a few minutes.

"Where's Princess?" I asked, more suspicious than ever.

"She wanted out. I think she wants to investigate what's going on next door. So far there's a car and a red truck over there that don't belong to you."

My throat tightened, my distress deepening. "Could you see them? Could you see what was going on?"

"Not really, I just saw the vehicles. I didn't see the guys. Doesn't that red truck belong to the good looking guy?"

"Good looking?" I was momentarily stumped. "Oh, you mean Mike. He's attractive, I guess. I wouldn't exactly call him good looking. But James, please bring Princess in. I don't let her wander around outside. I'd go myself, but..."

"She'll be all right," James said, turning and looking out the back window. "You always told me I was handsome."

"I'm not sure what you mean. I don't believe I've ever said anything like that." Goose bumps tingled my arms as the hairs stood up on them.

"I believe you know you were Elene Page in your past life."

250

"I think I was. But how do you know that? I don't understand. Where did you get this information? Who have you been talking to?" My voice rose as I focused on his crystal sphere.

He walked over to the chair where I sat, standing behind me, putting his hands on my shoulders. He stooped and spoke gently in my ear, his words nearly hypnotizing me.

"Suzanne, I saw you coming long before you ever bought the place next door. I've been here waiting for you, knowing our time would come again.

"When I saw these two Victorian houses, it triggered something in me—especially when I saw your place. In dreams, I saw snatches of scenes, and I knew I had been here before, that *we* had been here before.

"Then I learned about scrying, and this crystal ball found me, and the story of Michael and Elene became clear."

"Crystal clear," I said, a glimmer of understanding flickering through the foggy agitation in my brain. "This isn't fair, James. I'm not ready for all this. I have jet lag. Can't we wait until later? I'd be glad to talk about all this tomorrow."

The hands tightened on my shoulders and all reason and mercy sank away somewhere far outside my reach.

"This is the perfect time, Elene."

"My name is Suzanne. What do you have to do with Elene and Michael? What is it to you, James?" My heart thumped again, and I hoped my intuition would be proved wrong. This was all a bad dream—my night terrors returned.

251

He came around front, still maintaining his hands on my shoulders, his body now obstructing any hope of escape.

"But don't you remember? Don't you know who I am? I recognized you right from the beginning." His hands were squeezing and beginning to hurt me. "I was Michael, your husband, and you were Elene. I've seen it all in my crystal ball. We can be together again. You wanted to be together, didn't you?"

His hands relaxed slightly. "But what became of you after you killed Elene?" I said, fascinated by the story in spite of my distress.

"It wasn't murder. I would have never killed you. I loved you beyond anything else."

"But I saw Michael killing Elene. I saw it. I know it happened." How could I be a part of all this madness?

"I just lost control, that's all, with Victor and that business. I lost control, then I didn't know what to do, so I put your body in the woods and killed myself.

"But why are we talking about all this old stuff? This is a reunion. We should be rejoicing." He pulled me up and held me tenderly in his arms. My body tensed, rigid and riddled with fear.

"Relax, Elene," he whispered into my ear. His hands were beginning to roam over my body.

"I'm Suzanne. Suzanne Westin and I've got to go home. I'm very tired and I have to get straightened up from my trip.

You're frightening me and your name isn't Michael, it's James."

"I'll go over home with you," he said into my hair. "We must never be apart again. It's our second chance."

I tried to wrench free, feeling trapped and victimized. "Let me go. Please let me go."

"Sing for me, Elene. Sing me something pretty." He held me so tightly that I could barely breathe.

"Let me go." The harder I struggled, the tighter he clamped me against him.

"You can't go with him. I won't let you. You're mine."

"I won't go with him. He's long dead and gone," I said, hoping to break through his delusion. "James, for God's sake, let go!"

"I can't. I won't. Victor can't have you," he said quietly and simply. I felt instant relief as he released me for a second, and then his hands tightened around my throat.

A horrible gurgle filled my ears—my own death rattle.

Chapter Twenty-Four

*A*ll my psychological training drained out of me as the breath left my body. I operated purely on a primal level now.

He's going to kill me. Yet, I couldn't manage a whisper, let alone a scream, and I could barely resist him now.

A picture formed in my brain. I saw Princess, alert and focused, coming into the house, bounding up the stairs, teeth bared.

Come, I called to her in my best telepathic form. *Princess, come.*

The room grew dark as I began to lose consciousness, just as I heard a noise downstairs. Was it her coming?

Help, Princess, I called silently as my final effort.

"What the hell?" I heard him yell as the hands, those life-choking hands were wrenched from my throat.

James was screaming at Princess, and I hardly believed the ferocious growling and snarling from the dog who had always been gentle and loving. She lunged at him again and again, teeth bared, whenever he tried to make a move, with blood splattered on his pants and shirt—hopefully his and not my dog's.

"Get her off me," he yelled, glaring at me.

I feared James might hurt Princess just as I heard steps and shouts on the stairs, and I held back, knowing more troops had arrived.

Mike and Brad took one look at the situation, then dived in, pinning James to the floor. Princess padded over to lick my face.

"Get out of my house, all of you," James commanded from his face down position. Somehow, none of us were convinced by his authority.

"What's going on, Suzanne?" Brad asked. "What did this guy do to you?"

"He tried to kill me. He was choking me. I was losing consciousness when Princess hurtled up the stairs."

"That's what we saw. Your dog was visiting with us as if we were long lost friends. All of a sudden, she ignored us and sat up tall, as if she heard something, then she rushed next door and bashed her way through the screen door. The inside door must have been cracked open." Mike looked concerned even now as he spoke. "I just figured you were over here, and it looked urgent. When we got inside the house, we could hear shouting and snarling."

"Why did he try to kill you?" Brad asked from on top of my attacker.

"I didn't try to kill her. It was just a misunderstanding," James said.

"Right. A misunderstanding caused those bruise marks on Suzanne's throat. You be quiet," Mike said.

"To answer your question, I've known I was murdered in a past life from my crystal ball gazing and past life regressions. I thought it might have been you, Mike, because his name was Michael and he looked exactly like you." As the truth slid out, relief washed over me.

"The guy who murdered you looked just like me? That's pretty creepy. No wonder I couldn't get you interested," Mike said.

"But James here remembers that past lifetime, said he was the Michael who was my husband, who murdered me in a jealous rage. He said he remembered everything. He had been gazing into his crystal ball long before I moved into my place. I guess my winning personality in this lifetime hasn't convinced him to forget the past."

"Suzanne, if these two guys would leave, you and I could work this out on our own," James said, his voice convincing and reasonable—again the neighborly helpful guy.

I coughed, my throat still hoarse from the trauma of James's hands.

"I don't think so, James," I said. "I don't think I'll ever trust you again. Some things are mighty hard to forgive, and I've certainly never harmed you in this lifetime."

"Oh, but you hurt me beyond human comprehension when you were Elene. How can I forgive that kind of behavior?"

256

"You don't sound very innocent to me, buddy," Mike said. "By the way, what are we going to do with this guy? I don't know about you, Brad, but I'm getting tired of sitting on him."

"I have to go to work," Brad said, "although if I'm a little late it'll be all right. I guess we should call the police."

"I'd like to see him put away somewhere. He's too close for comfort living beside me on this hill," I said and dialed the local number with shaking hands and explained the situation as best I could.

We hear sirens within a few minutes. Three police cars with flashing lights pulled up behind James's place. I ran downstairs to let the officers in.

"Are you Suzanne Westin?" asked the officer in charge, a man in his thirties in black uniform with 'Officer Ryan' on his name tag. Two other policemen stood behind him as I held the screen door wide. The bottom half of the screen door had been ripped out from the force of Princess's body as she had entered and now flapped free.

"Yes, I am. We have James Rummel upstairs. Two of my friends are holding him down. He tried to strangle me. Please come in."

They eyeballed my throat, what was left of it, and nodded to each other and then followed me up the stairs. As we entered the bedroom, I could hear him calling out.

"Officers, these people are trespassing in my house. They do not have my permission to be here. They are holding me against my will. Please arrest them."

257

"You say he tried to kill you by suffocation?" Officer Ryan said and turned to me, and touched my throat. "Your neck looks pretty convincing."

"He used his hands. I came over here to get my dog, and the dog and my two friends ended up saving my life."

"Looks like we'd better lock this guy up and take him in for questioning," Officer Ryan said. "Any reason why he attacked you?"

"He thinks I'm some woman from his past—another lifetime. He says he killed me in that lifetime and he was trying to kill me again," I said. What I didn't say was that I had seen it all happen myself, in my crystal ball. I feared Officer Ryan wouldn't believe me, and I needed help. James was too far gone for me to be safe with him living next door.

"Sounds mental," Officer Ryan said. "Hallucinations. We'll take care of all this. Can the three of you meet me at the police station?"

James was handcuffed and pulled to his feet, his face at best a study in suppressed rage. One police officer checked for active bleeding, but James's wounds were mostly nicks. Princess, who had been hovering at the fringes of this scene, trotted over and licked his hands as though nothing had happened.

I felt a stab of remorse, for this was James, my friend, the man who had taken care of Princess in my absence. None of it made any sense.

James's face softened. "You're still my girl, Princess. I forgive you."

"I forgive you, too, James," I whispered.

The police led him out. Brad decided to drive separately since he had to go to work.

"You afraid to ride with me, doll?" Mike said.

"Not any more, now that everything's clear," I said.

"So you thought I was your enemy," he said.

"I wasn't sure. You look exactly like him, Elene's husband who murdered her in the 1940's. I never suspected James. James has been only kind and helpful for all the months I've known him."

"The boy next door?"

"Exactly—he was wholesome and helpful, and literally, next door."

"Maybe there is no boy next door, Suzanne."

"I know. This is how I felt when my cousin told me there was no Santa Claus."

We climbed into Mike's red truck and he backed out to make the short drive to the police station.

"Say, I ran out without my wallet and I see I'm almost out of gas. Can you loan me ten dollars?"

I smiled tiredly and fished through my purse for my wallet.

For once, I didn't mind handing over the bill to Mike. I just said aloha to my money, knowing it would never come back to me from Mike's direction. I'd be forever in his debt.

Chapter Twenty-Five

This was Monday, December 22, the winter solstice, the shortest day and longest night of the year. I was celebrating in the flower gardens in front of my house, of all places, for though the temperature was a frigid thirty-five degrees, we had no snow on the ground. My hands numb in the gardening gloves, I was clearing out the debris in the beds in preparation for new growth next spring. I'd gotten behind with my trip to Kauai right before Thanksgiving and James's arrest.

But today, the sun wasn't holding back, illuminating the pristine sky like a celestial cheerleader. Though the day might be short, the sun burst out gloriously, and I knew the light would be returning now, each night inching shorter, each day stretching longer until summer solstice.

Somehow, the heaviness in my heart was eased by the return of the light.

Frantic yelps replaced the earlier, intermittent barks of Princess, whose tie-out spot was behind the house. She knew I was somewhere else, and she wasn't tolerating separation from the pack. I walked around back to ease her suffering and to keep in the good graces of my remaining neighbors.

She whined and leaped at me, and I smoothed her shaggy fur. "I can't let you wander out front, sweetie. You not only saved my life, but you're my best friend in this strange, confusing world."

I stooped down and hugged her to me, facing the big old Victorian next door. The place seemed lifeless without James's presence. Locked and shut up tight, not a hint of movement anywhere, nor a creature stirring within its walls.

"He's gone, Princess, locked up tight like his house. I'm not sure what's going to happen to James. It's all up in the air, but for now, we're safe."

I shivered. *I'm not sure I'll ever feel safe again.*

The legal wheels were turning, but what would happen to James was still a guess. It had been nearly three weeks since his arrest. My newly-acquired lawyer said James wouldn't be released until after his trial, if even then; the bond would be high. He said the trial would take place in six months to two years. The charge of aggravated assault carried a longer sentence than attempted murder. But the news didn't console me, for I was convinced he'd be out soon, that somehow he'd be released.

And he'd be back in the twin Victorian beside me, still nursing a decades-old grudge against someone I used to be.

A breeze rattled the brown leaves on an oak next door, and the sound comforted me and brought me back to the present moment. Princess stared at me with those brown, intelligent eyes, her furry silvery black head cocked to one side.

"We'll go in, girl. Too much thinking out here."

She bounded in the back door beside me. I was altogether too aware of the darkened house next door. I carried with me a strong conviction that I must leave this house that I loved so much.

I sat in my dining room with a warming cup of herbal tea, savoring its delicate orange aroma. Princess flopped on the floor nearby.

"Too much thinking in here, Princess," I said.

Lately I had been imagining Elene Page and her husband Michael in my house. It was as if they were haunting me. Shortly after Teddy's warning, I'd done a title search for the property, but their names were never on the deed. I suspected they'd rented the house.

I considered checking old records to verify their deaths, even searching for and visiting their graves. Yet, I had verification enough by occult means, and the souls who had been Elene and Michael Page were no longer in those graves. I was weary of the entire scenario, yet I thanked Teddy every night for crossing back to warn me.

My lovely Victorian, my peaceful retreat and an oasis in a world of troubles, was again the site of my nightmares.

I still slept all night, but in the morning I'd awaken feeling James's hands around my throat, his nails digging into my neck. In one variation, I dreamed I was dancing with Victor in Elene's Victorian, and Michael sprang at us from every doorway of the house.

Now I walked through these cherished halls and sensed stillness, a waiting, anticipation—waiting for the other shoe to drop, waiting for James to come home and murder me.

I had trouble sitting still these days and hoped the change was temporary, for I needed to sit and listen to my clients. I often fought the urge to run, yet I had nowhere to run to, anyway.

"Far, far away from here, Princess. That's where we need to go," I said, and she seemed to understand. She could make the transition to anywhere as long as she was by my side. "After all this business with James is over, I think we'll go."

A wooden Tiki god, bought on Kauai in the hotel gift shop, guarded the floral centerpiece on the dining room table. I picked him up. The small black wooden guy had green eyes that glittered. I read "Kanaloa, god of happiness and eternal joy" on his base.

Happiness and eternal joy sounded just about right.

I sat in the dining room chair fingering the wooden statue as the green eyes glowed up at me. They reminded me of Teddy's eyes, and I recalled his words to me about the pattern of my past lives. Could the lethal cycle have ended? Would I be able to love and be loved?

Since I got home from Kauai, I'd tried calling Sam a few times, but had gotten his answering machine. Perhaps our attraction had just been a vacation thing, I'd told myself, and so I hadn't left a phone message.

But this afternoon, gazing into Kanaloa's sequin-bright eyes and musing on the concept of far, far away, my thoughts zeroed in on Sam Pahinui and his beloved Kauai.

Suddenly, I knew, and a peace settled throughout me. I could find a normal life again, a better and even more fulfilling life.

I rattled in the buffet drawer looking for his phone number. It magically appeared.

My hands were shaking as I picked up the phone and pressed it on. I stared at the receiver as if it were possessed, for a voice talked at me, though there'd been no ring.

"Is someone there?" I asked, almost expecting to hear from Elene Page or her Michael.

"Suzanne, I've been trying to reach you. All I get is your answering machine." His voice flowed clearly across the miles, and I sensed some tension behind his words. The aloha spirit flowed around me as I heard his voice.

"Sam, I've called you, too. I just now turned the phone on to call you, and you were on the line." I hesitated a moment. "I guess there are no coincidences."

"I should have left a message, but I wasn't sure if you'd want to hear from me. I thought maybe I was just a holiday friend. But, Suzanne, I've been worried about you. What has happened?"

I poured out my story of James, his attack on me, and his subsequent incarceration, and how fear crouched behind every corner of my house now. I aired my concerns that James might be released and my life would again be in danger. I tried to tell my story without emotion, yet my voice grew hoarse as I finished my litany.

He paused as if trying to absorb the situation. "I'm sorry, Suzanne, sorry you had to go through that." Then his voice brightened. "So you're coming to live on Kauai? You're calling to tell me you're coming?"

"The legal stuff isn't over yet, and I'll need to sell the house, but yes, I want to come and I guess I just wanted to hear you say you were still my best friend on the island."

"Oh, I could do better than best friend, dear wahine. But don't worry about selling the house. Just grab that dog and a swimming suit and come. It's time to get you out of there before anything else happens. You can fly back for the trial when the time comes. I'm sorry I wasn't there to watch over you when James went berserk."

"You've done plenty, my friend. I'll come back to Kauai just as soon as I can." My gratitude welled up and I was afraid I'd start crying from joy.

"After you left, Kauai just wasn't the same," he said, his voice hushed, then he cleared his throat. "You must promise me one thing."

"What is it, Sam?"

"No more brother and sister stuff between beautiful mainland psychologist and heart-struck island psychologist."

"I miss you so much. My feelings are entirely unsisterly, and I don't think there's any way back," I said, wishing I could wrap my arms around him right now.

He sighed in relief. "I agree, my hula maiden. And don't forget that every day there are rainbows on my island."

"And on Kauai, nature will take its course, won't it, Sam?"

"Especially on Kauai, fair wahine."

The End

IF YOU enjoyed this book, please post a review on Amazon, telling others what you liked about it. This helps others to find my books. Many thanks!

AND you might be interested in the Lilith & the Faeries Series, designed to help the reader connect with the nature spirits. Expect romance, fun, and adventure, with some faeries sprinkled in. See the next page.

AND don't forget to get your FREE *Tales of the Wild & Seldom Seen* E-book. Go to **www.CathyACorn.com**

Thanks for reading!

THE FAERIES ARE HERE TO MAKE YOUR DREAMS COME TRUE!

BLUE MOON OVER MADAGASCAR
Lilith and the Faeries Series #1

Pittsburgh bookstore manager Lilith Devlin meets a faery in her garden, who asks her to write a book explaining faery ways and to tackle a special mission. In exchange, the wee one promises romance and adventure.

Though Lilith fears change, she soon travels to Ireland to learn from the fae, meets an attractive New York editor, and flies to Madagascar with him to stop poachers from destroying endangered lemurs. Her world expands in unexpected ways as she grows closer to the faeries and discovers the mysteries of nature ...and love.

Available at: Amazon, Barnes & Noble.

ADVENTURES IN PARADISE

SMELL THE PLUMERIAS
Lilith and the Faeries Series #2

Lilith and new love Adam relax on the Big Island of Hawaii, a "free" vacation from the faeries, until a beloved dolphin friend is murdered. As they investigate this tragedy, they unveil an even more disturbing mystery: who is invoking the wrath of Pele, volcano goddess?

Amidst increasing volcanic eruptions, earthquake tremors, and threat of tsunamis, they race to solve these puzzles as they seek to grow closer to nature, this island paradise, the faeries, and each other.

Available at: Amazon, Barnes & Noble.

THIRD IN THE TRILOGY
A test of their love for each other

FAERY: THE FINAL FRONTIER
Lilith and the Faeries Series #3

The faeries contact Lilith and Adam about the Dream People, a tribe in a remote, mountainous region of the Ecuadorian rain forest. The tribe meditates to heal the world, and nearby oil drilling threatens their mission.

Lilith, Adam, and four shamans explore the forest to find the one man responsible. As a further challenge, Lilith and Adam's love must be tested to solve the mystery.

Available at: Amazon, Barnes & Noble.

CAN A PAST LIFE HOLD THE KEY TO HER PRESENT ONE?

The Witch's Lost Love

Stephanie Gray joins a group of women to find her roots, for she has drifted in her jobs, where she lives, and especially in her relationships. The Women's Healing Circle introduces her to a way of living close to the earth, as Wiccans did years ago.

But when Circle member Flo turns up missing, Stephanie discovers an eerie connection to a previous life that puts her present one in mortal danger. Can she leave the past behind and find love and happiness now?

Available at: Amazon, Barnes & Noble.

Acknowledgements

*W*riting has enriched my life in so many ways. When I first published this novel as an E-book in 2011, I had such a thrill seeing my work in print. I am eternally grateful to the folks at Smashwords for helping me realize my dream.

The words continue to fascinate me and the process of how they magically appear on the pages. I am grateful to all my muses and spirit guides for the work. For I find such joy in it and hope my readers do, too.

Learning to write has also been a fascinating journey, and I've met such wonderful souls along the way. I've belonged to writers' groups, gone to conferences, taken Community College courses. My critique partners helped shape my voice.

Story is powerful, pure and simple. When life has us down and out, we can read these stories and find escape. But over the years, I have also learned that writing stories can change our reality. I studied the work of Lewis Mehl-Madrona, MD, PhD, and am convinced if we change our stories, we can alter the very fabric of our lives.

I want to thank the faeries and other nature spirits who are teaching me about a world full of joy and light. We can learn to take care of Mother Earth and play more.

Nature's ways and creations are more exciting than any action-packed Hollywood drama. We need only learn to be still and wait for the magic to happen.

So don't be afraid to write your own stories, especially to rewrite those parts of your life that are burdensome and keep you from your highest good. You will find that there are more hours in your day and that all becomes lighter and more fun.

Namaste.

ABOUT THE AUTHOR

Cathy A. Corn, RN, RM, MT, lives happily-ever-after in Pittsburgh with husband Alan and critters Cato and Cleo. She practices massage/energy work and speaks and teaches about the faeries. Her study of healing spans many years and still fascinates her more than dusting furniture.

Learn more and sign up a free book for joining her mailing list at **www.CathyACorn.com,** where she blogs about healers, healing, and the wonders of the natural world. You can also touch base with her on her Facebook page, Cathy A. Corn, writer. She believes your dreams can come true—don't you?

And don't forget to go outside and visit the faeries.